HONEY WHISKEY MURDERS

Also by Staci Mercado
SEEKING SIGNS

Honey Whiskey Murders

Staci Mercado

Four
Feathers
Press

FIRST EDITION

ISBN 978-0-692-98840-4

1. Historical Fiction—Iowa—1920s. 2. Thriller—Fiction.
3. Iowa—Fiction. 4. Prohibition—Fiction. 5. Detective—Fiction

Four
Feathers
Press

Printed in the U.S.A.
10 9 8 7 6 5 4 3 2 1

For The Don

Amendment XVIII to the Constitution of the United States

Section 1.

After one year from the ratification of this article the manufacture, sale, or transportation of intoxicating liquors within, the importation thereof into, or the exportation thereof from the United States and all territory subject to the jurisdiction thereof for beverage purposes is hereby prohibited.

Section 2.

The Congress and the several states shall have concurrent power to enforce this article by appropriate legislation.

Section 3.

This article shall be inoperative unless it shall have been ratified as an amendment to the Constitution by the legislatures of the several states, as provided in the Constitution, within seven years from the date of the submission hereof to the states by the Congress.

Elsie Edens
Saturday, November 4, 1922

As a private investigator, you must live inside a case—see it, smell it, get your hands dirty—then, and only then, do you really know what you're up against. Most of the time, things aren't too complicated, but every once in a while you'll come across a situation that throws you for a loop.

Take the Brownfield case, for example.

Sit down for a minute. Imagine this.

Homer and Rosela Brownfield, ages 43 and 41, respectively, are murdered in their country store. He lies behind a long wooden counter that nearly stretches the length of the place. Mr. Brownfield is tall, perhaps six feet or more. A small dog is perched on his chest and growling but skitters off when you approach. He has an ice cream scoop in his lifeless hand, vanilla pooled and congealed on the floor next to his blood; the two substances curl into each other, maintain independence until collapsing into a cherry cream. The entry wound is on the left side of his forehead. There's no sign of a struggle. In fact, Mr. Brownfield's revolver is holstered at his side. Another is stashed underneath the ice cream tub. A large wad of cash bulges in his vest pocket. Then you look down the counter and see that the cash register is still full of money—a fair amount for stealing if one was in for that sort of thing.

Mrs. Brownfield's body is in a back room. The state of her face and head indicates she has been beaten to death. The bodice of her dress is bloody and ripped open, stockings torn. A small handgun lies on the floor near her. The sheriff tells you Mr. Brownfield died sometime before midnight last night, between nine and ten is his best guess. Mrs. Brownfield, however, didn't pass until the next morning, nearly twelve hours after her husband.

In an adjacent back room, Diamond flour coats the floor, spilling from a large hole burst in the top of its cloth sack. A dozen bags of baking goods still rest on a shelf along with other stocked provisions. There are two sets of footprints; Mrs. Brownfield's is smooth with a pronounced heel. Another print is wider with a light tread. Not Mr. Brownfield's work boots, you note. Each set leads to the closed window. At the base of the window, most of the flour is dispersed, evidencing a clash of wills.

Though both bodies are on the first floor, the second floor contains clues as well. A set of stairs leads up out of the room that Mrs. Brownfield's body is in, and at the top of those creaky steps there are four bedrooms. Three of them are untouched by trouble, as far as you can see. No drawers or trunks have been ransacked, nor is there anything of interest left behind, but in the last bedroom on the left, a struggle has taken place. The mattress of the bed is askew, so much so that the bottom corner touches the floor. Noticing that the side of the mattress has been ripped, you look closer and find a woman's fingernail dangling from the fibers. The bedclothes are thrown aside and several hairpins litter the mattress. There is dried blood on the bed and specks on the wall. In the corner of the room is a man's dress shirt, spattered with bloodstains on the shirtsleeves and chest. You are certain this shirt is not Mr. Brownfield's; he is a large man, and the shirt is at least two sizes too small.

The other clues remain outside, though most are ruined. Someone set fire to a wallet, a logbook, and some miscellaneous papers. The morning rain came in and doused the fire, resulting in half-burnt and soggy materials. The only item worth salvaging is the logbook, so you wrap it in a handkerchief and stash it inside your coat. If the perpetrator wasn't looking for cash, what was he looking for? And did he find it?

What are you to make of all this? There is so much hidden in the tableau at your feet.

I wasn't new to the detective business, but I suppose I looked like it. At only 22 years of age, I had actually been around the block a few times and then some. Unfortunately (if you look from one angle), and fortunately (if you look from another), I was ready for the case.

My mentor's encouraging words rang in my head: *They don't know what you're capable of.*

I turned off the main highway and onto the county road that connected the small towns of Low Moor and Elvira. It ran just in front of the country store, not twenty feet from the front door. My first thought as I approached was that with the occasional traffic, someone must have seen or heard something—lights, cars, or gunshots.

By the time I pulled into that dusty drive, the entire sheriff's department and half of Clinton County, Iowa, was there for a look-see. Model T cars and Selden pickups were parked alongside horse-drawn wagons and buggies, all crowding the small lot.

The biting November wind did not invite the shedding of my long wool coat, so no one noticed my revolutionary attire. Emboldened by the changing times, I had recently given up dresses and skirts for good. Not only were pants more practical given my profession, but they also felt more *me* somehow.

I wove through throngs of thrill seekers who craned their necks attempting a glance at the scene inside. Women, men, and a few children had abandoned an otherwise busy Saturday, one normally reserved for trips to town, in favor of the new drama that unfolded. They whispered of murder, rape, and theft.

The building was a long rectangular structure, two stories tall. The lower level served as the business, while the top had been a living quarters for the deceased. Two red metal chairs sat on the low porch on each side of the front door. On each side of those, unmarked crates and barrels covered the porch floor, preventing the onlookers from getting any closer. A young deputy stood before one of the chairs maintaining a comical look of attempted authority, his chest puffing out like a strutting rooster.

"This is a crime scene, Miss."

"You don't say?" I placed my hands on my hips.

"Step down from the porch now. We have work to do here."

"I'm Elsie Edens."

"And?"

"I'm here to help."

He chuckled and looked out at the rest of the people gathered behind me. "Just what do you think you're going to do?"

I pulled a hard leather case from my coat pocket and opened it. "Here's my card. I work for the Phinneus

Lawrence Detective Agency. We've been hired by Mrs. Brownfield's sister to look into her murder."

"The sheriff's department's looking into it."

"And so are we."

"Where's your boss?"

"Mr. Lawrence isn't well."

"What makes you think——" The deputy was cut off by someone shouting through the screen door.

"Let her in, Mandersheid!"

Chagrined, the deputy opened the door for me; for a split second his upper lip rose in a sneer. "Don't lose your breakfast in there. It's not pretty."

Sheriff Ramsey met me at the door. "You must be Miss Edens." The new sheriff's cerulean blue eyes were slightly disarming. He was an attractive man, with black hair greying at the temples, brow permanently creased down the center. "Mr. Lawrence called and said you were on your way."

"You're not put off by my presence?" I asked.

"I'm not nearly as concerned about who gets the credit for solving this thing as much as I am about getting justice as quickly as possible."

"You didn't inherit a tight ship."

"That's the truth of it. I'm well aware of the reputation Clinton County has, and one way or another, I'm going to turn that around. Let me show you what we walked into here."

In those early days, my profession benefitted from such loose regulations. I'd never be allowed into a crime scene now. Ramsey was a step up from his predecessor who was known for allowing concerned locals into a crime scene, just as the investigators had in the small town of Villisca.

Ten years earlier, the bloodiest crime in Iowa happened there. Two adults and six children were murdered with an ax, and to this day they haven't figured out who did it. After

19

the doctor examined the bodies, dozens of onlookers rushed in, tramping through the house and destroying much of the evidence. There just wasn't a tradition of excluding the community back then. Locals were trusted observers and helpmates to overworked and under-qualified authorities not well-versed in the art of investigation. Unfortunately, there were also many who were there as thrill seekers and gossips. A piece of the father's skull was on display at the local pool hall just days after the murders.

Unlike that fiasco, Ramsey kept the public out but was still open to private help if that private help knew what they were doing. He and Phinny had rubbed elbows a time or two, so I was trusted not to mess things up at least.

The sheriff walked me through the scene while I took meticulous notes. I have to tell you, I'll never be able to eat vanilla ice cream again. When I see it, I see Mr. Brownfield's blood mingling with the melted cream on that wood floor and smell its sweetness together with a metallic, coppery tang.

Someone had closed Mrs. Brownfield's eyes, but the terror of her final moments was forever etched in the arch of her eyebrows and the jutting line of her jaw. That terror seeped from Rosela Brownfield and found its way into me regardless of distance, regardless of profession. It woke some sleeping thing I hid in my closet but so desperately wanted to understand.

When I was younger, I often played at investigation.

I would worry the corner of my notebook with my thumb and imagine.

The blood. It's spattered everywhere in the attic—on my lazy-eyed china doll, Mother's green typewriter, the worn leather suitcase I took to

St. Louis, and on my brother's infant shoes. It saturates the floorboards, pools in the knots.

I write: single victim.

Mother comes up the stairs; she doesn't see any of it because the crime scene breathes only in my imagination—a dark menacing creature. The smell of it refuses to leave me. Its coarse hair sticks to the threads of my wool coat.

When she asks what I am doing, I don't answer because the reality of it is exactly what she doesn't want to hear, exactly what she is trying so hard to forget.

Somewhere behind my father's old accordion is a lock of my sister's hair. It's supposed to be in mother's cedar chest, but I use it as evidence. She can't see it from her vantage point, so that real thing stays to play the game.

Mother is afraid of the answer to her question and doesn't pry further. With each of her slow, descending steps, she sends a message of concession.

I draw a body on the floor with a stick of chalk—trace it around the blood. The body is much bigger than mine, so when I lie down in the frame, its edges protrude far beyond me. The outline is the same size and shape as the one I saw dead in another place many years before, when it wasn't a game. I run my finger along the border of the space and it catches on a sliver, but I don't bother to pull it out, for it's something to feel.

Another real thing is the knife hidden underneath a blanket, stolen from father's memory box. That token will be my protection later—beyond dreaming—but in this time and place, it only plays a part.

Two years after I graduated from high school, I found myself knocking on the office door of Mr. Phinneus Lawrence, Private Investigator. The daily drudgeries of helping out at Mama's hotel, the Farmer's Home, and being courted by inane local boys had driven me to seek the excitement I so desperately needed.

I had met Phinny when I was a kid. Before he settled in Clinton, he stayed at Mama's hotel for a spell. After several days of serving him coffee, we struck up something of a friendship. He told me about his profession and gave me some literature that inspired my investigation into my sister's murder.

The eleven section booklet led me right to her killer, but the part labeled "Self-Defense" did little to protect me from him. My friend Walter and I nearly died.

Though Phinny had been gone almost a decade, I'd never forgotten him. He moved his business to Clinton after years of a transitory practice. I wasn't aware of his move to the area until I found his business card left behind by a hotel patron. I knew it was a sign. I needed something more, something real, something raw. My past had made me unfit for a normal life.

Phinny was a short-statured man with a pear-shaped figure. His wispy black hair threatened to abandon its post altogether, but maintained small patches of resistance to age.

After two weeks of constant pestering, he had agreed to take me on in the capacity of mentee until I tired of the profession and came to my senses. I promised him that wouldn't happen. After six months, Phinny finally decided I was suitable for more than a seat at a desk, and began taking me out in the field.

On a brisk fall morning, the mysterious death of one Hester Tate brought three women to Phinny's door. She had no family, so her girlfriends took up her cause. They were certain they knew who the killer was, but they had no evidence to prove it. The three local ladies pooled their money and sent Phinny to Minneapolis to have a look at the suspect.

I never did have the heart to tell Phinny about the trouble I got into with that one. It was one of the first cases he let me help him with, and I didn't want the circumstances to cause him to say I told you so—or worse, to fire me out of guilt.

Against Phinny's better judgment, I had volunteered as bait. I dressed like the dead woman, a young flapper in a short skirt, and walked into the speakeasy alone. A jazz band played on a wooden stage and white people danced alongside colored couples on the floor. Exhilarating. Never would have seen that back in Iowa. Not in those days.

One gin fizz later I laughed loudly at the bartender's jokes and caught the eye of my prey. My t-strap balanced on the end of my toe while my crossed leg bounced. Feigning mishap, I flung the shoe to the corner, and there he was— right on cue. He stooped to pick it up and returned it to my stockinged foot along with a gentle caress above the ankle.

He had a pin stripe suit and a sweet face—almost sweet enough to convince me to let down my guard for a second— almost sweet enough to make me forget Hester Tate.

I poured every gin fizz after my first one into the spittoon at my feet as he ran his pinky finger along my forearm and listened to my fabricated story of a neglectful and abusive husband.

The plan was to lure him to our rented room in Minneapolis after closing time. There he would confess; Phinny would make sure of it.

Despite the proximity to dangerous sorts, I enjoyed my profession. It allowed me to keep people at a distance for the most part. I watched them, listened, examined—only interacting if I chose to, and when I did choose, that interaction was on my own terms. That was the beauty of it—the beauty and the lie.

As we passed an alley, he grabbed me around the waist and whispered into my ear. "I know what you want." He yanked me into the darkness, and I remembered that old booklet. "Expect to get into dangerous situations," it said. "What should you do when you have to protect yourself?" Good advice, but only experience taught me self-defense. I'd been through this kind of violence before. I knew how to protect myself.

He tried to take control. He wouldn't listen. He wouldn't stop.

It wasn't so hard for me to stick the knife in him, just above the belt line in back, not as hard as I imagined—that pop of skin like a soft, ripened fruit.

I surrounded his body with empty grocery crates labeled Lake County Bartletts, Golden Sceptre Oranges, Royal Club Cherries.

A chilly rain started, a cleansing wash that numbed as it rinsed all traces of that moment away, filtering them deeply into some earthen place that transformed those traces into pure energy—neither good, nor bad, and no longer a part of me.

I told Phinny the guy never showed that night. I had been secret keeping all my life. What was one more?

The next day a stray dog uncovered his body, but his murderer was never found. The papers read, "Another Unjust Murder in Minneapolis."

Hester's case was closed when Phinny searched her murderer's apartment and found a bottle of chloroform and several ladies' handkerchiefs, one embroidered "HT."

Even though my father's knife saved me that night, afterward I had a strong desire to get rid of it. I cleaned it a dozen times, but each time I touched it, I felt his warm blood oozing between my fingers. Each time I looked at it, I felt his hands running up the inside of my thigh.

Now the river carries that knife along where it mingles with catfish in the murky depths and tickles the underbelly of the city.

Now it's buried in a foot of mud.

Now it's held in the roots of a fallen tree.

Now it's washed out to the sea where it's pounded and pounded by the salt and surf until it is nothing—nothing at all.

I bought a new weapon after that. "Something deadly," I told the shopkeeper, "something unexpected." It was that, all right—a double-sided switchblade. No matter which end came out of my pocket first, there was a blade ready to spring. I kept it clean and well-oiled, just as I had watched my father do with his knives and yard tools many years before. I would always be ready.

Phinny's office and adjoining apartment were on the sixth floor of the Wilson Building, the tallest one in Clinton. Its steel frame structure was covered in a white terra cotta finish. Hundreds of box-elder bugs clung steadfastly to the south side, sunny and bright on one of the last warm days of the year.

I preferred the stairs to the necessity of conversation with George, the curious and chatty elevator operator, so when I entered Phinny's office, I was slightly winded from the climb.

Inside the door sat Phinny's desk, a smaller version for me, and straight-backed chairs for clients. His parrot, C. Auguste Dupin, fluffed his feathers inside a cage placed just before the tall windows, soaking in the sun. Behind Phinny were numerous newspaper articles from the Midwest—crimes solved with Phinny's help. Everything from robberies to murders. He'd done it all, though the bulk of his career was used up by tracking counterfeiters.

"You know," Phinny said, "the elevator is easier."

"For some, maybe. You know me."

Phinny stuck a sunflower seed just inside the parrot's cage. "George isn't a difficult man. Just talkative."

"Nosy, some might say."

"Not everyone who asks questions about you is nosy. That's what some people call friendly." He smiled, his crow's feet reaching prominently across his temples.

C. Auguste Dupin snatched the seed from his fingers.

I took out my notepad and pencil and laid them on my desk before taking off my coat. Several sheets of paper stuck out from my desk drawer. It was crammed with stuff, useful and not. My drawers at home were just as messy. Out of sight, out of mind, I guess. I never could stand a lot of things on my desktop, though. Visible Clutter got in the way of clear thinking.

"What did you find out at the Brownfield store?" Phinny asked.

"It wasn't a robbery, that much I know for sure."

"Oh?"

"At least not in the typical sense of the word. There was quite a bit of money left behind."

"Was anything else missing?" Phinny began taking his own notes.

"I'm not sure, but it seems like the motive may have been to cover something up. I found things someone tried to burn in the back yard." I reached down and pulled out the leather-bound logbook from my coat. "This survived." A cloying smell, like that of burned hair, wafted from the book and several cinders fluttered to the top of my desk. I handed the logbook to Phinny, then bent down and blew the cinders to the floor. Wiping ash from my fingers with a handkerchief, I said, "I haven't scrutinized it yet."

"Let me look through it. I can do that here. Let me be of some use."

"How's the arthritis?" I didn't know until many years later, but Phinny suffered from rheumatism, a disease that tortured him to no end and forced an early retirement.

"Miserable. It'll only get worse as the weather gets colder. I'm ready to go south. What else do you know?"

I showed Phinny the sketches I made of the crime scene—the locations of the bodies, the weapon underneath the counter, the state of the bedroom upstairs.

Phinny's phone rang. I examined the sketches as he carried on the conversation, which was clearly on the subject of Rosela Brownfield.

After a brief discussion, he hung up the phone. "Get over to the coroner's office."

I rose, pulling on my coat. Phinny grabbed a sleeve and pulled me toward him. His hands shook with discomfort.

"It's likely the person we're dealing with here is not an amateur. You have a gun yet?"

"You know I don't." It was a sore subject between us.

"A knife's not going stop a man with a gun, Elsie. It might slow him down, but it won't stop him."

"You've told me that before."

"I know, but you haven't listened yet."

As I walked out the door C. Auguste Dupin croaked, "Be careful out there."

There was no medical background necessary for a coroner in those days; Kellogg had been voted into his position. Many of the unsolved cases in Clinton County were due to the coroner's incompetence. Nine years earlier he had ruled my sister's death a suicide, despite much evidence to the contrary.

His office was detached from the hospital, just across a narrow alley and tucked between two storage sheds. The three rickety wooden steps suggested the need for repairs, but the brick structure itself was in fine shape.

I parked and reached into my handbag for a handkerchief and a tiny vial of lavender oil. I doused the cloth liberally, a trick suggested by Phinny to mask the unpleasantness of death. I'd never attended an autopsy before, and though I was slightly nervous at what my physical reaction would be to the gore, I was also excited more than I liked to admit.

Handkerchief in hand, I knocked on the door, but it wasn't Kellogg who answered. He was a young man, perhaps in his late thirties. His white smock was stained with blood, and several wisps of brown hair had found their way out of the cloth covering his head. "Can I help you?"

"I'm . . . you're not who I was expecting."

"Kellogg's out of town. I could say the same about you."

"I'm Elsie Edens, hired by Pearl Bohne, Rosela Brownfield's sister." I handed him my card.

He raised his eyebrows, horizontal wrinkles spreading across his forehead. "Doctor Rutherford. I'd shake your hand, but . . ." He gestured at the mess behind him.

"You're a doctor here?"

"Just started in August. I moved back after studying in New York. Family's here."

"I've heard about what Charles Norris is doing with forensics there. Did you study with him?" Norris and his partner, Alexander Gettler, were using new scientific methods to bring justice to a system rampant with conjecture and rotten with politics. Every dead body held clues. Norris and Gettler learned how to read them.

"Indirectly," Rutherford said. "I've heard his lectures. 'Cyanide Poisoning and the Body.' 'Mercury's Effects on the System.' Fascinating, gruesome stuff."

"We could use that kind of scientific thinking around here."

"Science is smarter than guesswork, that's for sure." Dr. Rutherford stepped back and motioned for me to come inside.

Mr. Brownfield lay on a table in the back of the room under a white sheet; his bare feet protruded from underneath it, and he was missing two toes on his right foot. The skin covering them was unmarred indicating an old incident.

Mrs. Brownfield's covered body lay in the center of the room on the main examination table.

"There's nothing to be told about Mr. Brownfield that we didn't already know. Shot in the head at close range. The bullet entered the left side of his forehead. Dead immediately. Mrs. Brownfield is a different story," Dr. Rutherford said.

As I approached the table, my foot struck a metal bucket filled with a clump of bloody rags. I brought the handkerchief up to my nose and gazed too long at the mess inside.

Rutherford peered at me over the ridge of his oval spectacles and resumed the explanation. "Upon initial examination at the scene, it seemed that she had been beaten to death." He grasped the sheet, but hesitated. "Are you ready?"

I nodded and bit my lower lip.

Pulling back the covering, he revealed Mrs. Brownfield's entirely cleaned out skull. The scalp had been separated from the cavity and folded down over her face. The removed skullcap sat alongside a bone saw and a metal bowl held her brain. Several areas of the organ were saturated with blood.

"The damage was so severe it was difficult to tell the exact cause of death. Whoever did this to her used a blunt instrument of some kind to cause a large amount of damage to the face and head, but that wasn't what caused the mortal wound."

"No?"

Rutherford turned to the table and picked up the bullet he had pulled out of Mrs. Brownfield's skull. "This entered her right nasal bone; the bullet was angled upward, so I'd say the shooter was Mrs. Brownfield's height or possibly shorter."

"Time of death?"

"Mrs. Brownfield didn't die of the wounds, exactly. She would have, but in the interest of mercy . . ."

"She was still alive this morning?"

"She was still alive when I arrived, yes."

"Did she say anything?"

"She was breathing heavily but unable to speak. Her death was inevitable. I administered morphine to ease her suffering. She died at 9:04 a.m."

I wondered if Rutherford's dose of morphine was premature. Would it have been possible for Rosela to give some kind of response? "And Brownfield?" I asked.

"He'd been dead for quite some time. I'd say nearly twelve hours prior."

"So much time in between," I muttered.

"I can tell you it's not what you might think." Dr. Rutherford covered up Rosela's head and pulled back the sheet to reveal her thighs. "There's no bruising, no lacerations or evidence of forced—"

"He didn't rape her?"

"The state of her clothing had me thinking otherwise, but no."

"Can you determine a time on the bruising?"

"I can only approximate. Most of the bruises occurred many hours before she was shot, especially the one I found on her head."

"Anything else?"

He held up one of Rosela's hands and ran a dull blade underneath a fingernail, extracting a rusty mass of dried blood and skin. "Someone is marked by her; there's no doubt about that. She put up a fight."

"There's something to look out for then."

"The official inquest will be tomorrow. Kellogg'll be back then, but what I'm telling you, you can take as fact."

Tino Cerone

My mother wasn't really a mother. She left me on a doorstep like in one of those Charles Dickens novels—not that I've read any of them myself. The Vulture read them to a pack of us at the boys' home. That was her only tenderness. Outside of book reading, she was a mean old bird.

She always used to say, "Watch what comes from above, Tino. Something is coming for you." I don't know what she was trying to tell me, but occasionally I look up, wondering. What kind of thing is that to say to a little kid?

The home was always hard up for cash. When the wealthy remembered, we'd get donations of books and food, toys for Christmas. Conscience cleared, they'd forget about us for a year or so. Usually the Vulture scraped by, rationing even the dregs. I didn't hate her, though. She ate no better than any of the rest of us as far as I could tell. Skinny as a rail.

We survived like that until I decided to take matters into my own hands. I realized, at age six, that there was a gold mine of produce and other food available right on the street. I began by taking just an apple or two a day, hoarding it for myself or wolfing it down quickly in an alley before going back home. When I got real good at it, I took all sorts of things and hid them under my bed.

Hard to find a good hiding place in a boys' home. Someone ratted.

The Vulture didn't ask me where the food came from. Didn't need to. Just pulled out a knife and sliced up small sections for each of us.

This went on for years and then I upped the ante. I'd taken to pickpocketing. Easiest thing in the world is to take a man's wallet right out of his back pocket.

My biggest score came on the day of a parade. I was maybe ten, eleven. A brass quartet marched down the street and someone on a unicycle tossed salted peanuts into his mouth while circling the band. I don't remember what the parade was for, but it was hot out. The men didn't have jackets on, so picking was even easier than usual. Too easy. I had three wallets in my bag when I eyed a more challenging target.

He stuck out from the rest of the crowd, had little interest in the parade. Wore a white suit of all things, rings on his fingers, had a gold-handled walking stick. Four men flanked him and the crowd parted for them. The man held a walking stick under his left arm, waved at a few people here and there with his right.

I ran out in front of them, purposefully tripped and sprawled, skinning my knees and hands bloody. Got to make it look good if you're scheming. Women and men stirred around me, jockeying for position so they could keep watching the parade. One of his men yanked my arm and stood me up.

In the fracas, I reached into the back pocket of his white pants and tucked that fat billfold into my bag before anyone could say boo. I looked up at him and he looked down at me.

His brown eyes didn't really see me, looked through me more like, and there was a tiny crumb of bread on his thick brown mustache. Without a word, I turned and ran through the crowd but felt his walking stick thwack the back of my legs first.

That was the biggest day I ever had as a pickpocket. Just a little shit and I had over $240 in my bag.

By that time, I'd found my foolproof hiding spot. There was a loose tile just behind the claw-foot tub, not easy to get to, but it worked. Before that day, I already had $72 in there.

That act, taking that particular man's wallet, was what changed everything for me.

His men found me a couple hours later. I had squirreled underneath my covers and was counting my money while the rest of the boys were scavenging the mess left behind by the parade. The Vulture walked the men right up to the room and lifted the blanket off me before I knew what was happening. There I was, with a fat wad of cash—not just his, but all the money I'd taken.

One of them took me by the ear while the other snatched the cash out of my hand. The Vulture wrung her hands and followed us out the front door.

"What'll you do to him?" she asked.

"That'll be for Mr. Colosimo to decide," said the man who had my ear.

I didn't know who Colosimo was at the time, but I found out soon enough. He was the single worst person in the entire city of Chicago to steal from.

I knew about houses of prostitution, but I sure as hell had never been in one. I got an eyeful that day. We walked down a couple blocks, up one, right in the front door where Colosimo sat with his white suit at a big round table covered in cash. Two women stood by his side. One had bright red hair and smoked a cigarette. The other had a black eye and

her dress hung loosely around her breasts as if it had been ripped. Seated at tables were several other men with barely dressed women on their laps.

Colosimo pointed a finger at me. "Stand there and don't move until I tell you," he said.

So I did. Arms at my sides all afternoon. The only thing on me that moved was my eyes, and boy, did I see a new side of life. The money came in like water from the pump. Thirteen men delivered cash that day, dumped it out on the table, and I watched those stacks get higher and higher, mouth-watering at the thought of it.

Evening came and the sun set. The woman with the black eye lit the lamps and served Colosimo a big plate of pasta and sausage. I swayed on my feet and had a powerful urge to piss, but I knew I was being tested, so I stayed.

Colosimo ate slowly and when he was finished, he soaked up the rest of the sauce with a slice of bread, downed the last of his wine.

My stomach growled.

The woman with the black eye came back to clear his plate.

"You want what I got?" he asked me. He reached out and grabbed the woman by the arm. She cringed and nearly dropped the plate.

I didn't know if it was right to say yes or no to that question, so I didn't answer at all.

"Cash, women?"

I nodded my head.

"You'll work for me now, and someday, you play your cards right, you'll have it."

The Vulture had never raised a hand to me before that night. When I returned, she sat at the kitchen table with a bottle of whiskey. Never knew her to drink. I stood before her, waiting for harsh words, but what I got was a licking with a wooden spoon. Thwack, thwack, thwack. It went on for so long the boys upstairs got out of bed and peered down the steps to see what was going on.

The next morning, we woke to a rich breakfast, the likes of which we'd never seen. Pancakes, bacon, eggs, and oranges. Never had an orange I didn't steal before that day. I assumed that was her way of making up for the beating she gave me the night before. I learned later that Colosimo's men delivered a crate of food to the back door before any of us was up. That became a regular thing. The crates came with a price, though. The Vulture's boys became the eyes and ears of Colosimo's operation. All in all, cheap payment for the hours we put in, but we didn't know any different. We didn't care. We were fed. We had a place. We were needed.

Elsie Edens
Sunday, November 5, 1922

Because I rant not, neither rave of what I feel, can you be so shallow
as to dream that I feel nothing?
—R.D. Blackmore

It wasn't my sister Minnie's killer we were burying. It was me. I was both burying and buried somehow. You know how dreams are. They rarely make sense. You scramble for a foothold, then the whole damn rug is swiped out from under you; you are upended, and you land in another space altogether, a space both familiar and wholly unrecognizable all at the same time.

Minnie's husband and my brother John pulled my body from the back seat of the car. I was wrapped in a rug soaked with blood, bound in a tarp to keep the moisture in, rolled up so tight not even my fingers had room to move. I tried to cry out—to tell them I wasn't dead, but I was unable to make a sound.

The scream within me was suppressed by a greater good—a need to protect the family. No one could know what we had done.

Each man had taken an end of the rug and they swung me back and forth, gathering the momentum necessary to toss my clear conscience into the pit.

While the dirt piled on top of me, worms burrowed into the folds of my prison, and I felt them chewing the ends of my fingernails.

Then another me—I felt the weight of the earth on the shovel, the liberation as I flung dirt on top of him, gradually covering his dark hair, his olive skin, his bad intentions.

The moon winked out, then returned with a blinding ray of light that washed out all color. I knew I was no longer myself, but something altogether necessary—both caretaker and deceased.

When we were through burying him, we walked away, leaving the old me behind.

My mother placed the morning newspaper next to my plate of eggs and bacon. The headline read "Coldest-blooded double murder and robbery in the history of Clinton County." A smattering of Mother's hotel costumers dined in the far corners of the room.

I absentmindedly played with my switchblade below the table. It helped me think.

"Do you have to do that here?" Mama asked. "It makes the guests uncomfortable."

No one paid me any mind as far as I could tell. The customers' faces were buried behind newspapers or focused on their food. Rarely did anyone interesting wander into the place. Most of the men who stayed there were farmers traveling across the Mississippi, purchasing cattle in Illinois and shipping them back to Iowa or fattening them up in Iowa and shipping them to the stockyards in Rock Island. Occasionally a colorful fellow would wander in and cause a stir, but mostly those who wanted something on the wild side had plenty of other places to choose from. Either way, I certainly wasn't worried about what any of them thought of me.

Having hired help for the hotel, my mother didn't need me to work there anymore, but the Farmer's Home was the perfect hub for my work. I had the ability to come and go as needed, could walk to the office, and could keep an eye on my mother.

My many nieces and nephews secretly called Mother Little Fat Grandma, for she was a mere five feet, and nearly as wide as she was tall. As she looked down at me in my chair, she said, "You're not getting involved in this one, I hope."

"No, Mama." Mother didn't need to know what she didn't need to know.

She narrowed her eyes. "Whatever happened there, you can bet it was tied to liquor."

"Why do you say that?"

She rested her hands on the table. "There are a lot of people in and out of this hotel. I hear things."

"Is that so?"

"Yes, but it doesn't matter to you, since you don't have anything to do with this case."

"Right, Mama."

COLDEST-BLOODED DOUBLE MURDER
AND ROBBERY
IN THE HISTORY OF CLINTON COUNTY

—

COUNTY OFFERS REWARD OF $500
FOR EVIDENCE IN BROWNFIELD MURDER

SHERIFF AND POLICE SEEKING CLUES TO IDENTITY OF MURDERER OF TWO

INQUEST IS TODAY

CORONER CONDUCTING INQUIRY THIS AFTERNOON—MOTORISTS REPORT TO AUTHORITIES—TELL OF FORD COUPE PARKED NEAR BUILDING ALL NIGHT.

Through Sheriff C.L. Ramsey, the Clinton County board of supervisors today authorized a reward of $500 for information leading to the arrest and conviction of the murderer or murderers of Mr. and Mrs. Homer Brownfield, who were shot to death in their wayside store on the Lincoln Highway at Low Moor Corners, about six miles west of Clinton, late Friday night or early Saturday morning.

Today, Sheriff Ramsey and the Clinton police were still without tangible clues as to the identity of the murderer. Whoever shot Mr. Brownfield dead, apparently did so as Brownfield stooped to wait on him. He also fatally wounded Mrs. Brownfield, who died at 9:04 o'clock Saturday morning, about an hour after Peter Wilden, a

40

customer, entered the store and discovered her unconscious and dying in a pool of blood.

The sheriff and police are running down various clues furnished by motorists who passed the store during the night and early morning.

Nearly all the reports of passing motorists indicate that the store was dark after 9:30 o'clock Friday night. One motorist, who passed the place between 9:20 and 9:30 o'clock, reported that the lights were burning, that Mr. Brownfield was wrapping bundles and that Mrs. Brownfield was seated in the middle of the store.

Another who passed the store at 9:25 o'clock reported that the store was dark at that hour. A motorist who passed the place at 10:45 o'clock declared that the store was then dark and that a Ford coupe was parked on the east side, headed toward Elvira. One motorist, bound for Low Moor at midnight, observed that the lamp that usually hung from the ceiling of the front entrance porch was down on the floor, the auto's headlights being reflected from its nickeled surface.

It is therefore believed that the attack took place about 9:30 o'clock and that the murder of Brownfield was followed by the darkening of the store by the assassin or assassins who pulled down the lamps, possibly with the intention of thus firing the building.

Their stories give further basis to the theory of Coroner Kellogg that Mrs. Brownfield was not shot until hours after the death of her husband, basing his belief on the nature of Mrs. Brownfield's wound and the loss of blood, which he declares would have caused her death within a few hours and long before her death occurred, if she had been shot at about the same time that it is believed her husband was killed.

Numerous false reports were in circulation yesterday and today concerning the murder mystery. One report was to the effect that a message had been received here by radio telling of the arrest of three men in Omaha for the slaying. Another, circulated today, was to the effect that a man residing in Clinton County had been arrested. The sheriff denied both reports.

Mother and I spent entirely too much time together. She'd developed the ability to read my thoughts, even when I tried hard to hide them from her. Maybe it was my body language. She could always tell when something was up. I don't know why she suspected I was looking into the Brownfield case, but she was right, of course.

I paused on the hotel step long enough to see one of the town's eccentrics, Louise, peering out from a fourth floor window at Van Allen's Department Store. She had the strange habit of looking at everyone from the corner of her eye, head lowered. She sometimes growled. It made her look like something of a menace to those who didn't know her well. She never hurt anyone, but acted like a wild animal, though she could read a bit. I knew because I was her desk partner for the second grade. She attended only up until third grade when her unusual characteristics were too obvious to be ignored anymore. Her mother pulled her out of school to help in Kline's, the family's general store. Louise

never waited on customers, only dusted and stocked shelves while patrons gave her a wide berth.

When her mother died several years later, the business was passed on to relatives who were supposed to take care of Louise, too, although it didn't really work out that way. Louise's aunt was kind to her, but that didn't make up for the cruelty of her uncle, who had little tolerance for her unusual behaviors. Bruises emerged on her neck and arms.

When I was sixteen, stories of the haunting of Van Allen's Department Store emerged. During the early morning and late evening hours, employees heard strange creaks and moans coming from somewhere overhead. Stories began circulating about broken items being fixed and floors being cleaned overnight by some unseen specter. The four-story building was something of a marvel to the community, being fully equipped with washrooms, electricity, and a fresh-air exchange system. Originally, the noises were thought to be caused by the modern amenities in the store. Modernity made noise, but there were still some things no one could explain.

Then an employee arriving early discovered Louise on the second floor at 6 a.m., trying on a woman's coat. That employee, in an attempt to impress his boss, had planned on getting the day's sales all laid out and tagged before his boss arrived to tell him to do so. He did not plan, however, on *not* being the first arrival in the store that day. The first arrival was someone who actually never left. Louise had made a fine nest for herself in a corner of an unused portion of the fourth floor, where, according to rumors, she had likely taken up residence for nearly a month before she was discovered.

The authorities were called that morning, and just as the city police were walking Louise out the door, Mr. John Van Allen himself arrived for work. He was told that a vagrant had set up residence on the fourth floor and attempted the stealing of a coat from the women's department. Mr. Van Allen could have pressed charges, but such was not his way. It had been said of him, much to the chagrin of some of the well-to-do snooty ladies of the hill, that all customers looked the same to John Van Allen. The wealthy stood in line with the poor, the servant girl with the millionaire. A dollar was a dollar no matter whom it came from, but more importantly, a person was a person. The owner and founder of Van Allen's Department Store walked Louise away from the police that day and gave the ghostly handywoman a job. Mr. Van Allen understood that Louise just wanted to be useful.

Mystery solved, Louise didn't need to work out of sight anymore, but she never shed her odd habit of skulking and growling at people, no matter how hard Mr. Van Allen tried to teach her. Louise was happier if she could do her jobs away from the public. Anyway, there were certain workings of the store that John Van Allen didn't want the public to see. Those things did not include Louise, but rather the fine-tuning of his modern marvel. Van Allen knew that as soon as the wonder wore off, business would slow down, so Louise waxed floors and maintained the general behind-the-scenes necessities that made the building continually new and never broken. Like magic.

One untenable part of that arrangement, however, was Louise's choice of accommodations.

Mr. Van Allen arranged for Louise to stay at Mave's. Mave ran a café from the street and a speakeasy from the alley. She had rooms available upstairs and a need for someone to act as lookout in the event of an oncoming raid.

Shortly after Prohibition took hold, speakeasies had emerged in the cities and towns. They were foxholes of brick and mortar, in deep, dark places—a haven to the crazy world beyond. To hell with that damn law, people thought.

Police rolled in on speakeasies when the politicians and hatchet women were in town, just to make a show of it. Local police went back to their ways once the dust settled and broke out their own stashed bottles as well. Shady stuff happens when someone tells people no.

Mave's place had been modest before Prohibition, but liquor laws bathed her in a much-improved income. During Prohibition, people drank more, not less. When Prohibition became law, she bought a heavy door, hired a burly doorman, purchased an assortment of spirits from the Midwest, and made a killing. Louise only added to her security. If the authorities were coming, Louise simply flipped a switch that caused a red light to appear over the bar, and every drop of alcohol was poured down the drain or stashed behind a secret door.

Louise was needed. She received free room and board for her services at Mave's, and Mr. Van Allen made sure the money she received for working at the store was managed. She received a weekly stipend for expenses and the rest of her money was put into the bank.

I waved at Louise who placed her hand on the window. I had saved her from schoolyard bullies more than once back in the day.

C. Auguste Dupin began barking as soon as he heard my key in the door. Phinny had taught the bird to sound like a large dog in order to scare away potential trouble. Not only did it succeed at that, it also annoyed the hell out of me. I could never tell for sure whether the thing was actually as smart as it seemed, or if some of the things it did and said were just pure coincidence. If Dupin was hungry, he didn't care who was coming in, but if he was content, he chose to

45

make others miserable. Phinny tolerated it all, and never scolded the bird for any rudeness.

Phinny was a great fan of Edgar Allen Poe and named C. Auguste Dupin after Poe's fictional detective who first appeared in "The Murders in the Rue Morgue." The fictional Dupin was a gentleman; unfortunately, the bird version was boorish.

C. Auguste Dupin wouldn't stop barking until I told him to shut up, upon which he replied, "Go to hell."

"You've made that thing into a monster, Phinny."

"He entertains me."

C. Auguste Dupin interjected with a very human sounding cackle. Instead of being locked in his cage, he was perched on the edge of Phinny's leather chair.

"I may be on to something with that logbook," Phinny said.

"What is it?" I settled into my desk.

"Brownfield had taken to lending things, money and goods for those who couldn't afford it."

"Debt could be motive."

"That's right, but there's also another possibility." He handed me the logbook. "See what else is there."

"What is it?"

"Take a look; see if you can figure this one out."

I saw Phinny's point about money owed to the Brownfields. Many locals racked up a deep tab at the store. Some of that debt was for goods purchased, but Brownfield also obviously lent cash to those in need. There were no extraordinary amounts, however—nothing that pointed to murder as the only way out.

A separate section of the book dealt with shipments delivered to and from the store. Phinny laid down his calendar. There was a significant difference between the style of the entries recorded Mondays through Thursdays, compared with some of the entries recorded Fridays and Saturdays. Most of the week, thorough records were made of amounts, goods, names, and locations. While dollar amounts were recorded for Fridays and Saturdays, an ambiguous coded system was used for some incoming and outgoing materials, names, and locations. Those debts were paid on both ends, but a lack of transparent records indicated a likely involvement with liquor.

"I can't be sure, but it looks like Brownfield was involved with some illegal distribution."

Phinny said, "That's where you start."

I couldn't shake the nagging feeling that I had missed an important clue at the crime scene. That one thing, like a single cricket chirping in a bedroom corner, seemed louder—more bothersome—than a chorus of insects harmonizing in the night. I lay in bed running through the details given by those who passed by the store on Friday.

Charles Y. spotted a car at Low Moor Corners just off the pavement and a short distance from the store sometime between nine and ten p.m.

Rupert B. stated that lights were on in the store at nine and off by 10:30 p.m.

Bill R. claimed that shortly after nine p.m. a truck drove away from the store at a high rate of speed.

Many witnesses spotted a Ford coupe parked at the store from 10:45 p.m. until approximately 6 a.m. the next day.

Clara W. heard a bang as she drove by the store early in the morning. Thinking she blew a tire, she pulled over. While she examined the vehicle, an unidentified car coming from the direction of Low Moor drove by going exceptionally fast. Her tires were fine. She wasn't sure, but she believed that a "dark-skinned fellow" was the driver. Her supposition was predictable. Those considered outsiders were often targets for unfounded accusations.

I suppose it's human nature to be distrustful of those considered outsiders, but it's unfortunate. Some groups learned to separate themselves from perceived expectations and go about life as usual, developing a tough skin, like armor. One such group was the German folk, who, in that area of Iowa, were common. During and after The Great War, Germans were often suspected of treason. When suspicions were turned over to the authorities, there were knocks on doors. Questions were asked. Two of my own siblings were questioned, as my family also came from Germany. No charges were filed, but it certainly put a scare into them.

"How long have you been in this country?"

"Do you still have ties back in Germany?"

"When was the last time you spoke to anyone there?"

"Did you fight in the war?"

"Are you involved in any plots against the United States government?"

"Do you consent to a search of the premises?"

Mothers and fathers sat around kitchen tables and wrung their hands while wide-eyed children looked down from stairwells. No evidence of treason was ever found in our area, only the occasional vat of home brew.

This xenophobia was not favorable for the German beer companies as it was one ingredient in the politics of Prohibition. Most saloons were owned by German or Bohemian immigrants. Moralists viewed them all as infidels who contributed to the demoralization of the population. Politician John Strange was quoted in the Milwaukee Journal as saying, "We have German enemies across the water. We have German enemies in this country, too. And the worst of all our German enemies, the most treacherous, the most menacing, are Pabst, Schlitz, Blatz, and Miller."

Other mistrusted groups included the coloreds, so when Clara W. reported seeing a dark-skinned man driving by after hearing what was possibly a gunshot, the attention of the authorities turned to known men of color in the area who were often suspected of trouble. For a long while, nothing of note came of the suspicion.

Despite the $500 reward, there wasn't much to go on, so I decided to drive the dark dirt roads in search of that thing or things I missed. I really should have told someone where I was going, but at that age I held on to a stubborn streak. There was no limit to what I could do—so I thought. No man who could outsmart me. No situation too cryptic I couldn't fashion it all out after a spell.

That attitude was a sign of the times. Votes for women! Those old chants rang in my head years after women had achieved the right, and I carried that torch so proudly my hands burned.

There's nothing more beautiful than an Iowa fall, and nothing more desolate than its aftermath. Stripped bare of all life by November, the fields reach beyond sight, an endless flat desert, raped of possibility. There are few trees to slow the wind; those that remain cling steadfastly to life but endure a lonely existence. Their only companions, the transient corn and oats that cluster and dominate the fields, are gone by November, emigrated.

No life at all called to me on that Iowa night. The insects were gone, crops gone, few cars on the lonely road save mine. So when life emerged from the ditch in the form of a doe, I didn't see her until it was too late.

Phinny was always telling me that we see what we expect to see. Expect nothing; expect everything. The times I forgot that advice were the times I needed it most; isn't that always the way?

The doe and I locked eyes, or at least we seemed to. The headlights mesmerized her—so beautiful, that one rare sign of life in the November desert.

I stomped on the brakes in enough time to slow down but not stop, and the momentum of that old rattletrap crashed into the doe.

Bursting from the car, engine sputtering, the one remaining headlight picking up fine grains of field dust, I prayed the doe had galloped off into the opposite ditch when I wasn't looking, but she lay there, side heaving, eyes wild with fright, blood trickling out her nose.

I knew I had to move her, to save her from the indignity of the road. So that's why I found myself pulling a deer this way and that, taking turns with the front and back legs. I nestled her in the tall grass while her blood oozed and her breath slowed, then stopped altogether.

I crouched down and said some kind of prayer, though by that time I had no idea what I was praying to. I had fallen out with God, or, at least, other people's versions of it.

The silence of the November night gave way to a distant tick coming down the Lincoln Highway. Moment broken, I got back into the car with death's whisper on my shoulder. A car passed going the opposite way, filled with people about my age. Smartly dressed, likely boozed up, and on their way into Clinton. Seeing them only made me feel lonely, less connected to the light things in life. I existed on the outside of it all, looking in, under, and through, but never *with*.

Before going into the Brownfield store, I sat in the parking lot to get a sense of the highway and local traffic. In a ten-minute span of time, there were three automobiles that passed on the road. It was nearly midnight, so I figured the traffic must have been busier at the time of Homer Brownfield's murder.

When I stepped out of the car, I detected the far-off whine of a train. It ran through Low Moor, just a few miles from the store.

The moon offered enough light for me to approach the porch without stumbling. I pulled the matches I remembered from my coat pocket and lit the porch lamp. Attached to the front door was a notice, "No public entrance by order of the Clinton Co. Sheriff."

It was locked, so I needed the toolkit Phinny gave me to jimmy the door.

As soon as I opened it, the smoke from a freshly smoked cigarette reached my nose. I didn't have time to react before a voice broke from the back of the room—so far back, the light did nothing to reveal its owner.

"Is that you, Elsie?"

It's hard sometimes to match a voice to a person you cannot see, like running into a familiar face in an out-of-the-way location. You stare, knowing, but dumbstruck for a moment. You think, Is that really you? Is this really happening? The voice was something like that. I knew that voice; I trusted that voice. Hearing it caused confusion and calm all at the same time, but it wasn't until Walter Winkle stepped out into the light that I really knew it was him. I hadn't seen him in a long while and was surprised to find that he had grown into a man. His dark hair was close-trimmed above the ears, but grown long on top and slicked back with wax. He hadn't shaved in days from the look of it.

"Walter, what on earth?"

"That *is* you."

"What are you doing here?" I asked.

Lighting an interior lamp, he said, "I used to make deliveries for the Brownfields."

"You worked here? I had no idea." I hadn't seen him at the crime scene that day, nor had anyone mentioned his name.

"Just deliveries. I wasn't there a lot. You know," Walter cocked his head, "I haven't seen you in a long while."

"How long has it been?" After graduating from school, time had completely gotten away from me.

"Years. I heard you were working for Phinny Lawrence."

"I am."

"Who hired you?"

"Rosela's family. They showed up on Phinny's doorstep shortly after they received word. They don't have much faith in the sheriff's department."

Walter walked over to the counter and put out the stub of his cigarette in an ash tray. "I don't like the thought of you looking into this one."

"Why's that?"

"It's ugly, is all."

"Most of the things I look into are ugly, Walter."

I looked around the room, trying to gain some answer as to why Walter was there at such a strange hour. There had to be some logical explanation apart from the crime. "What are you doing here this time of night?"

Walter slowly lifted his right thumb and pointed behind his back. "I just left some of my personal things here. Thought I'd pick them up while no one was around. I have a key for the back door."

"You really shouldn't be here. You could get in a lot of trouble."

"I know."

"Why don't you go ahead and grab those and get on home, Walter. I have some looking to do here."

"I . . . all right. What would you think about getting together sometime? For coffee?"

I smiled. "I'd like that."

Walter began walking toward the back, then hesitated. "I . . . Oh, hell."

"What?"

"I'm not picking up my things. I'm trying to . . . erase something." Walter's eyebrows drew in and up while the corners of his mouth turned down.

"What do you mean?"

"Elsie . . ." He walked closer to me then and lowered his voice, as if there were others who could hear him, though we were entirely alone. "Ma's taken on a lot of debt. Quite a bit of it exists in a record book here somewhere. She owed the Brownfields a lot of money. I figured with both of them gone now, that debt would only benefit the bank or some relative who wouldn't notice it being gone at all. For Ma, for her good, I thought I'd get rid of those records, help her out a little."

"Those records are gone, Walter. Taken in as possible evidence. They might lead us to someone with motive."

"What motive?"

"I don't know. You don't have any insight about that?"

"I really don't," Walter said. "The sheriff talked to me about it yesterday."

"Brownfield was in the habit of lending money to a lot of people," I said.

"When people couldn't get a bank loan, they'd go to him. He wasn't a tough guy. People liked him."

"Why did he carry a gun, then? And stash another one under the counter?"

"Look at this place, Elsie. With no one else around, it's a target for thieves. The Brownfields had more than one run-in with people who tried to take them for all they had." Walter lit another cigarette. That simple gesture filled up the temporary silence between us. He pulled the smoke in deeply and exhaled to the side. "I guess my plan isn't going to work out like I'd hoped. I'll leave you alone."

"I'm sorry, Walter." I wondered if the Brownfields' deaths brought back old ghosts for him. He was the one who found my sister's body nine years ago. He would have been nine then. "It must remind you of . . ."

"It does. Though I'm glad I'm not the one who found them dead. I couldn't have taken that again."

The thought of being left behind by myself suddenly felt intolerable, and against my better judgment I said, "I'd like you to stay if you don't mind." Walter agreed to do so and stood in the lamp's half-light while I poked around behind the counter. "How long did you know them?"

"Three years."

"You must have known them fairly well then."

Walter twisted the watch on his wrist. "I knew them well enough to know they didn't deserve this."

"What did you tell the sheriff?"

"Wasn't much to tell. Nothing helpful."

"Did the Brownfields have enemies?"

"Look, I was just a driver. I don't know anything."

"Sometimes even the smallest of things leads to something big. If you think of anything at all that might seem unusual or important, let me know—me—not the sheriff."

"Got it. What are you looking for anyway?"

"I don't know exactly. I just have a feeling I missed something before."

In one of the second floor bedrooms—not the one where the bed had been found askew, but a room just at the top of the stairs, I had found Rosela Brownfield's journal. It rested underneath the mattress, a pencil stashed between the pages. Her last entry read:

A moment before sunrise, a thin layer of fog settled over the land, resting in the crooks of trees, wetting the songbirds still in their nests, and misting the green ditch grass yet to be bitten by frost. Spotted sandpipers keened in the bare fields, invisible to hawkish predators in the veiled light of day. I carried a lantern in my right hand and the greying basket in my left. Walking away from the coop with a dozen brown eggs still warm, I raised my head while taking a deep breath of the Indian summer air. My husband opened the back door for me and let me inside. "Coffee's on," he said.

While we sat at the kitchen table together, a train approached from the East, roaring as it passed.

"How's your back this morning?" Homer asked.

"Better after a night's sleep," I assured him; though it wasn't.

"I've been thinking," Homer said. "It's time for us to take a day off."

I raised an eyebrow. "A day off?" Honestly, we haven't had a real day off in years.

"Yes, you know. A day without work." Homer smirked at me.

"That sounds nice, Mr. Brownfield, but . . ."

"Now, none of that. I'll plan everything."

I rose from my chair, my breakfast plate half eaten. I rubbed my calloused thumb over his right cheek. "You do that, Mr. Brownfield."

The remainder of Rosela's journal had no discernible clues as to their killer. No mention of disagreements with customers or family, though Rosela didn't always agree with Homer's willingness to lend out their hard-earned money. Their marriage had been typical. Rocky at times, but mostly happy. They seemed too busy to quarrel, really.

It wasn't until I'd scoured the first and second floors that it occurred to me. There was no visible stairwell to a lower level, so I thought there must be a cellar entrance outside. "Where's the cellar, Walter?"

He shoved his hands into his pockets. "No idea. I don't think there is one."

I took the lantern and walked completely around the outside of the place, but no exterior door led underground. I did, however, notice that a single window in the foundation gave away the existence of a cellar space. The panes were curtained, so even in the light of day, I couldn't have seen inside. I gave a brief thought to prying the window off before I came to my senses and realized that though the entrance to the space wasn't obvious, there certainly was a cellar; I just needed to go back in and find it.

Walter stood in the doorway. "You find what you're looking for?"

"Not yet." Given the layout of the place and the gradual slope to the foundation, I knew the likeliest location for an entrance was in the back. The storeroom on the right was entirely lined with shelves brimming with dry goods. Its floor was still covered in the spilled flour, but all floorboards appeared intact. There were no carpets covering up sunken doors. Next to it though, was the room Rosela was found in. It served as a mudroom for the Brownfields, with stairs leading to the second floor. Coats and work boots hung from wooden pegs; rag rugs covered the floor. The floorboards seemed entirely fitted; none gave the slightest hint of a hidden entrance whatsoever.

"Even if there was a cellar, what do you think you'll find?"

As my eyes settled on the space sealed off below the stairs, I said, "Motive."

Product fliers covering the wall underneath the steps offered cures for supposed medical menaces. Mostly just things that made people feel self-conscious—freckle cream, dandruff ointment, halitosis rinse, and La-Mar Reducing Soap (wash away fat and years of age).

I removed each of the papers, gradually exposing a door and a little wooden knob.

"I'll be," Walter said.

"You had no idea this was here, huh?"

"No. None." Walter rubbed the back of his neck.

No more than a light tug was necessary to open the space, and it revealed a narrow set of descending stairs. Either recently cleaned, or well-trodden, or both, the stairs were dust free.

Walter followed me down as I raised the lantern before me. Nestled just at the bottom of the stairs were 32 wooden crates.

I grabbed a crow bar and worked the lid off one of them.

The top layer was indeed honey, packed inside four pint jars. Hanging from each one was a white tag printed with the image of a honeybee and the words "Wild River Honey." Below that layer, though, and packed underneath a thick bed of straw, was something very different. The similarly tagged jars were much too watery to be honey. I screwed the top off one. The mixture inside smelled slightly of honey, but also something spicy and strong. It was moonshine whiskey all right. There were twelve jars to a crate—something worth killing for.

"Did you know Brownfield was selling this?"

"Sure. He and every other store owner this side of Iowa."

"So much alcohol. You sure there was no bad blood over this?"

"Mr. Brownfield sold to farmers and small businessmen. Locals—people he knew."

"Who were his biggest customers?" The logbook wasn't going to be any help on that. I knew Walter had to know something.

"I can't say."

"Who was he getting it from?"

"I won't tell you that, either."

"Why the hell not?" I felt my face getting hot. Walter knew a lot more than what he was telling me. I wondered what kind of deliveries he actually made for the Brownfields.

"Anything you know is likely to end up on the sheriff's desk eventually. I won't give up good people and expose them to legal action. None of them did this."

"What's more important, protecting bootleggers or finding the Brownfields' killers?"

"You won't get any leads from me. If I suspected any one of them did this, you can bet I'd tell you."

"For God's sake, Walter." I gritted my teeth.

"You just have to trust me. I'm doing some poking around on my own. If I hear anything, I'll let you know first. I promise."

I took one jar so I could show Phinny what I had found and made a note of the total quantity in my notebook. Walter and I parted ways after I drove him to a truck that he had stashed a quarter of a mile down the road. The temperature had dropped considerably in the time we spent inside, and I shivered as Walter opened the car door, letting in a bitter wind.

"Be careful with this one," Walter said. "I don't know who killed the Brownfields, but I do know that whoever it was, they won't hesitate to kill again."

"What makes you say that?"

"Just . . . just the state of the Brownfields. I heard it was awful."

"What do you know, Walter?"

He lowered his brow. "I don't know anything, Elsie. Will you please just be careful?"

"That goes for you, too. Stay away from that place."

Walter shut the car door and placed his hand on the window briefly before tapping a farewell.

He wasn't willing to talk about the Brownfields' ties to liquor yet; I knew I'd have to keep working on him.

Though what Walter had planned in terms of covering up his mother's debt wasn't okay as far as the law was concerned, I could hardly blame him. I had learned long before that there were certain things that caused logical folk to look the other way. This was an underlying understanding most of the time. The government was respected, but not trusted. No one ratted; no one blabbed. They just didn't talk about the illegal things they knew of. Sometimes things got covered up so well they just became part of the landscape, and no one remembered them anymore. Like a hill you pass every day of your life but never really see.

A few months after my sister, Minnie, was murdered and Walter and I nearly lost our lives trying to find her killer, Walter was kicked out of his house in Elvira. He went to live with an aunt in Clinton. No one really talked about why. Those things weren't discussed back then, but I knew his father was not a kind man, prone to violence and such. His ma sent him to live with her sister. Ends up, he and I went to the same school then. This was difficult for me, given the fact that I wanted desperately to forget the day we nearly died. Every time I saw Walter, the memory of that afternoon came flooding back again. *Hiding under the bed. The footsteps—hard, heavy, mean. That man peering at us, crouching, sneering.*

When I turned 14, I had a bit of a fit about it. I was sitting on the gymnasium floor for a school program. A magician from Davenport showed us how he could pull daisies from ears and change the color of a handkerchief just by passing it through his closed hand. It may have been the fuss of grackles coming through the window, or the shifting wind, or the scent of ozone before the rain, but something triggered my memory of that day and caused it to flood over me. In my panic, I scanned the room for a clean exit, and I saw Walter. His face was transfixed by the wonder of his teacher sawed in half. It reminded me of the look on his face while we hid, forehead furrowed, mouth open.

Gasping for air, I ran outside and slumped out of sight behind a yew bush, my head buried in my knees. My body blocked out the world for a while; I couldn't hear anything, couldn't feel. I stayed like that long enough for school to be dismissed. When I looked up, Walter was sitting next to me. He held the magician's program in his hands. "Wonders never cease—Gordon Thurston—The Man Who Knows," it read. Sporadic drops of rain began to fall on us and dampened the words.

He put his small arm around me and we stayed there until the rest of the children were long gone and The Man Who Knows was no more.

After that day, I practiced a sort of avoidance. Seeing Walter was a trigger and I was bound and determined to keep my finger off. I needed to forget.

Sometime that next school year, I found another way to cope with my troubles. The way was unexpected—but at least it was a path, and I was no longer just slogging around in the quagmire, looking.

That's when I began setting up elaborate crime scenes in my room or out on the lawn. I made cornstarch paste for blood, asked my older brother to walk through it for footprints, and left behind other traces—a coin purse, hair, a comb, a cigarette butt. Then I imagined the story told by the things left behind. I pulled out my journal and wrote a tale to weave it all together, from chaos into order.

Some might have considered those pretend crime scenes a game, but I know now they were much more than that. From the outside looking in, I must have seemed crazy. Once, my

two best girlfriends found me in the middle of an imaginary investigation. Mama let them in the house. If she had known what I was up to, she wouldn't have. Chrissy and Melanie opened my bedroom door and screamed. Suspended from the beam was a thick rope, tied in a noose. The noose wrapped around a pillow that I'd covered with the lavender blanket Mama crocheted for me. It looked very much like a head and cape. Very realistic, if I do say so myself. Underneath was a chair, knocked to the ground. Elsewhere around the room I had set various other items. Mama's best kitchen knife smeared with strawberry jam rested on my nightstand. I had dropped a dab of jam in a basin of water and swirled it around so it looked a bit bloody. Sunbeams danced across its pinkish hue. I'd wiped my fingers on a white towel and tossed it to the floor. Though my mind saw blood, my nose remembered strawberry toast. I smiled at the strange juxtaposition as the girls opened my door. Screams, excuses, apologies.

The next day at school, they were polite to me but held back certain confidences. I didn't blame them. Chrissy and Melanie grew closer, and I distanced myself. I couldn't tell them about what really happened with my sister, Minnie. Even if I had, they wouldn't have understood. She committed suicide; that was what the papers had said, and though it was far from the truth, it was what our family needed everyone to believe. When someone has a secret that big, it's like a looming cloud. Every once in a while, the sun might shine around or through it, but the cloud never goes away, because the secret is still there. So a person can fool herself for a second, by playing a short game in the yard or laughing at the dinner table, and then she looks up and is reminded all over again of the reality of her past.

When I wasn't writing about crime scenes, I read about them in the works of Sir Arthur Conan Doyle. I read

Holmes's words over and over again, trying to glean meaning, direction, knowledge, because though it was all fiction, I was sure there was something profound hidden in the words—something that would lead me in the right direction. I knew from experience, that one of his quotes was entirely true: *"There is nothing like first-hand evidence."* Sherlock Holmes also taught me the liberation of staying emotionally detached. Holmes kept his distance. With distance, logic can be employed. With distance, one does not get hurt.

Becoming a private investigator really was not a choice, you see. It was either continue to play forgetting games or accept the ugly thing that lay inside me and work with it. Beauty and redemption hide in unlikely places.

Tino Cerone

There's really only one time I can remember something beautiful. A local celebrity, some opera singer, don't remember his name anymore, took four of us older boys fishing on his family's pond north of the city. Black-and-white dragonflies flew around the reeds and grasses. Two black cormorants dove for fish, disappearing for several minutes before coming back up. The other boys wanted more than anything to catch a fish and bring it back for The Vulture to fry up, but I couldn't take my eyes off those birds.

One second they'd be floating on the water, and the next—gone. I tried holding my breath for that long; sixty seconds was as long as I could manage, but they were down for a good twenty seconds more than that. Just when I thought they must be drowned, the birds would surface, sometimes with a fish, sometimes not. When they caught one, they ran on top of the water before taking off, circling the area several times before landing in a nest at the top of a large, dead tree.

There were at least three babies in there. Their beaks rose up when the adults returned with fish, raised all kinds of hell with their demands. The adults brought up the fish they'd swallowed and gave it to them just like that.

Eventually, one of the other boys took notice. He wasn't catching a thing and got bored, so decided to shinny up the tree and pester the birds. The opera singer was occupied with taking a fish off a hook and paid no attention to him. I knew what the kid was up to. A bad seed who was always looking for some kind of trouble. I yelled at him, warned him to get the hell down or I'd clock him one. He didn't listen. Just yelled down at me, "What the hell do you care?" and kept on climbing.

That's when I grabbed a good-sized rock and whipped it at him. I didn't think I'd hit him. Oh, maybe I did. I don't know. Anyway, it clocked him a good one on the head and knocked him right out of the tree. He survived, but had a cut the length of your pinky finger across the back of his head.

That was the end of the fishing trip.

The birds survived, though.

Elsie Edens
Monday, November 6, 1922

If you want to keep a secret, you must also hide it from yourself.
—George Orwell

I brought the jar of whiskey to work the next day so I could show it to Phinny.

"Ahh, the likely source of all the trouble. I wish you'd taken more." He winked and slowly screwed the top off. After sniffing the contents, Phinny took a large gulp of the stuff. He held the jar out to me, but I waved it away.

"If you're going to know *who* you're after, you better know *what they're* after," he said as a wry smile spread across his face.

I couldn't argue with that. There were no identifying marks on the jar itself. It looked just like each and every glass jar used for the home canning of garden produce, though the jars were usually filled with much less startling stuff. The bee on the tag, however, would certainly lead us somewhere in particular. I was neither friend nor stranger to moonshine whiskey, but knowing the concoction was likely involved in the Brownfields' deaths, it soured me to the idea of it. One smell of the stuff, however, and I knew that particular whiskey wasn't typical. I took a sip and noted its smooth, sweet taste, unlike any whiskey I had ever tasted.

"It's good, eh?"

I agreed. Surely the distillers had hit upon something unique.

Phinny told the sheriff about the stash of whiskey in the basement. Though we kept many things to ourselves, there were certain tidbits we turned over to the police. It was somewhat risky to admit I had snuck into the place without approval, but Phinny knew it was unlikely the sheriff would do anything about it. It was more important that we passed on what we knew. The new sheriff cooperated with us, so it was important we at least gave the impression of cooperation ourselves.

We spent the day making note of the names and addresses of everyone in the Brownfields' bankbook. Without a lead, I was going to start looking into every person who knew them, especially anyone who owned a Ford coupe. That afternoon, I headed over to the funeral, hoping someone or something interesting would be there.

A small funeral crowd gathered on the dry, fallen leaves that rattled and crunched under shuffling feet. Masses of soft grey clouds accumulated in the loftiest parts of the sky, giving people no hope of a ray or two of sun in the last hours of day.

Walter arrived as well, and he and I stood together in the back of the group. Though he was clearly agitated, continually scanning the crowd and grounds as if looking for someone, he looked dapper in his overcoat, dress shoes, and hat. He would make a fine man for someone, someday, I thought. I recognized he was handsome, but in the same way one notices many beautiful things she doesn't yet know she wants to have.

That biting November wind, greedy, unpredictable, snaked its way underneath my overcoat and I found myself thankful I had taken to wearing pants.

When the burial was over, Rosela's sister sobbed quietly into her handkerchief and was escorted slowly away by her husband. Those remaining gathered together in pods of gossip.

"Did you hear?"

"Can you believe it?"

"And poor Rosela, hours later. Can you imagine?"

"Hard to imagine someone got the better of Homer Brownfield."

Walter looked over his shoulder as he walked me back to my car. "I've got to get out of here."

I thought Walter was overcome with emotion, but something else was bothering him. "Have you thought any more about who might have done this?" I asked.

"Of course I've thought about it."

"And?"

"And honestly, I hesitate to tell you for fear that you'll get too close to something terrible."

"That's my job, Walter. I'm trained to handle terrible."

He pinched his bottom lip between thumb and forefinger. "Maybe so, but I think this might be a little outside your realm of experience."

"You don't know anything about my experience!"

"For crying out loud, don't go getting defensive on me. This is serious!"

"I'm very aware of how serious this is, Mr. Winkle. That's exactly why it's up to us to do something about it!"

Walter closed his eyes and breathed out. "We can't talk here. Mave's. I'll meet you at Mave's."

"When?"

"An hour. I'll tell you everything."

I went back to the office until it was time to meet Walter. None of the information we learned about any case could be discussed over the phone—too many ears at the switchboard. I told Phinny that Walter knew something, and I was heading to Mave's to find out what that was.

"I saved you some." Phinny winked while handing over the whiskey I had left there earlier, now reduced by a third.

"It's tasty stuff," C. Auguste Dupin said.

"Ask Mave about it," Phinny advised me. "She might know where it comes from. And by the way, the sheriff's not happy."

"Why is that?"

"The whiskey you found at the store isn't there anymore."

"You're kidding."

"Not a drop left."

The bird repeated himself. "It's tasty stuff."

There comes a time in most tough cases when, because of all the foul play you've exposed, things start to get a little hairy. Instead of taking the reins and meandering through the case, gradually exploring the lay of the land, you end up being the horse or the buggy. You don't know it at the time, but the thing is about to turn on its head. Instead of giving the one-ups, you are all of a sudden getting them.

Most of the time, as a private investigator, you are somewhat like a photographer. You hide behind veils, disengaged from those around you. Like camouflage, you blend in, non-committal. It's just that sense of moving around in this impenetrable armor that gets you into tricky situations. It's inevitable, the danger, but life lulls you into complacency sometimes, like a cruel witch who cradles and coos, only to unexpectedly toss you from her lap into a deep and treacherous ocean. She blows you a kiss and says, "Good luck, little one," and smiles.

I arrived at Mave's a little early so I could ask about the whiskey before Walter showed up. Phinny was right; she was just as likely to know the source of it as anyone else in the city. Knowing the source wouldn't necessarily point to the suspects, but it couldn't be overlooked.

Nights at Mave's, Louise served as lookout, but raids were rare. Despite the occasional need for precaution, people came and went from the back alley entrance with little trouble. They knocked on the back door, and a small eye-level slit was moved to the side by Nathan, a bearded and burly doorman who intimidated the locals and drank coffee like a fiend. I had been to Mave's often enough, both investigating and not, and I had never seen him without a cigarette dangling from his lower lip. He was generally calm when things ran smoothly, but if anyone irritated him with belligerence or disrespected Mave, that man could move like a bull through a crowded street. If someone acted up or acted out, out he went—the easy way, being yanked by the collar and allowed to walk on tiptoes—or the hard way, grabbed by the seat of the pants and tossed out the door.

Once I stepped inside, my eyes adjusted to the lack of light. Dim candles inside red glass globes sat on each table and lined a shelf behind the bar. Nine wooden tables and eight bar seats were nearly the extent of the place, save a small raised platform that hosted a local or traveling performer on Saturdays. Mave hosted singers, accordion players, fire swallowers, contortionists, and an assortment of other unusual characters.

The first time I had been there, I was keeping an eye on the future wife of one Mr. Harold Kind. Mr. Kind was to inherit a fortune thanks to his family's success in furniture, and he had a suspicion his fiancée wanted to marry him only for his money. Well, the man couldn't have needed much in the lines of intuition. This lady spent most of her nights in smoke-filled barrooms, laughing it up with just about any slick talker who walked in. Left with them, too. She might have been beautiful, but that lady was no lady. It was one of the easiest jobs I ever had.

There were seven other customers there at that early hour, three single men at the bar and a table with two couples just inside the door. I sat at a spot in the very back—the only location in the whole place that could be used to keep an eye on everyone. I never could enjoy a drink or a meal with my back to a crowd. If no one was behind me, there were no surprises.

Mave started a blues song by Mamie Smith, then sauntered over with a bar tray and a grin.

"Join me for a minute, Mave." I pushed a chair out with my boot.

"What is it?" Mave's red curls bounced as she sat down.

I put the jar of whiskey on the table and pointed at the tag. "You have any idea where this comes from?"

Mave glanced at the jar. "Couldn't tell you."

"You need to taste it."

"That won't—"

"Please, taste it."

Mave took the lid off the jar and sniffed. "Still can't tell you."

"For God's sake, Mave, drink it."

She took a small sip of the stuff and her twinkling green eyes looked at me over the top of the jar.

I didn't get to hear Mave's answer; Walter walked in the back door and came straight over to the table. Mave stood up and smoothed her skirt. She and Walter exchanged glances before he sat down.

"You're early," I said.

"So are you."

Mave brought over a couple of glasses half-filled with a golden liquid but did not linger. When I took a sip, I recognized that it was the same stuff I found at the Brownfield store. It was an answer at least. Mave did know where it came from.

"Before I say anything else, I want you to know I didn't intentionally have anything to do with what happened to Mr. and Mrs. Brownfield," Walter said.

"Intentionally?"

"Remember I told you I made deliveries for the Brownfields?"

"You said you worked for them, yes."

"You said that." His voice wavered. "I . . . I just didn't correct you."

"What the hell, Walter?"

"I run whiskey, Elsie."

"What?" I glanced at the other customers, but none of them seemed to be paying us any attention.

Walter lowered his voice. "The store was a main distribution point—one of many."

"Oh, for God's sake." I shook my head. Mave's was clearly one of those spots he delivered to. "When you said you made deliveries, I thought you meant groceries, not liquor."

"You're not the only one who has to make a living, Elsie. You chose to defend the law after everything that happened; I chose to break it."

"I defend *people*, Walter."

"In a way, I do, too. Prohibition is a sham."

"We agree on that point. Let's get to what you know about the Brownfields. What the hell is going on?"

Walter lowered his voice, though Mave's music made it impossible for anyone else to hear. "Friday mornings are delivery days. Last Friday I'm pulling crates out of the back of my truck behind Mave's when some Italian guy walks up and greets me, says his name is Henry Barzetti. At first I think he might be in for some trouble, but I don't see anyone else and he seems friendly enough. Next thing I know he's asking me where he can get his hands on a load of the whiskey I'm delivering. I tell him that's not for me to say. I'm just a driver. He hands me a twenty-dollar bill and says, 'Who do I need to talk to?' Well, there's a certain way my employers like to do things. They don't trust just anybody. If someone wants alcohol, they have to get it from a distributor. The distillers have to stay off the map. I told Barzetti he should meet me in that same spot at nine that night, and I would take him to a place where he could get some of the whiskey. He asked me for a single jar; he said he'd send it back to Chicago right away so his boss could get a whiff of what he'd found. I figured for twenty bucks I could spare that much.

"I met him and had him follow me out to the Brownfield store. It wasn't until he pulled his Ford coupe into the light shining from the store window that I saw his Illinois plates. I wondered what a guy from Illinois would want with Iowa whiskey."

"Ford coupe? Walter! Didn't you read the paper yesterday?"

"I read it this afternoon. I couldn't bring myself to read it yesterday." Walter lit a cigarette.

I got out my notebook and a pencil. "What did he look like?"

"Brown-haired, 20s. Not real tall, about your height. He had a dark overcoat, but a light-colored hat with a wide brim that shaded his eyes."

"Any distinguishing marks?"

"Nah. Decent-looking guy, I guess. Scratchy voice."

"So what happened?"

"He told Mr. Brownfield that he was from Chicago, that they were on the lookout for decent whiskey. He had found what he was looking for at one of the speaks on Second. No one was willing to talk about where they got it, but he waited for the delivery and found me easily enough. That's when I left; it was Brownfield's business at that point. On my way out, I heard Barzetti say he'd take some, and if the bosses were pleased he'd be back for more."

"That's it?"

"That's it."

"Why didn't you tell me this last night?" I asked.

"I thought Barzetti just wanted booze. He didn't need money; he had loads of it from the looks of him. Everyone was saying it was a robbery."

"It wasn't a robbery. At least not in the typical sense."

"The paper said it was."

"I know, but there was a lot of cash left behind."

Walter grabbed a chunk of the long hair on top of his head. "Jesus, Elsie. It's my fault they're dead. I led Barzetti right to them." He let go of his hair but didn't bother to straighten it out. A lock swooped off haphazardly to the side.

"Why would he want them dead? What motive would there be?" I asked.

"I don't know."

Mave wiped glasses down behind the bar, but watched us from the corner of her eye.

I leaned in closer to him. "Did *you* take it?"

"Take what?"

"The whiskey from the cellar."

Walter took a gulp of his drink and wiped his chin. "Yes, I took it. I've got no choice but to look after my own interests and those of my family. The law doesn't need it, that's for sure."

"That was an awfully risky move."

"I know. I just . . . I have my mom to think about. I'm all she has now."

"What in the hell are you going to do now?"

"I'm going to get out of here. I've stashed the booze and it'll stay there until things die down."

There was a long pause as we considered the possibilities. Behind the bar, a glass shattered on the hard floor and Mave swore.

"Elsie, I'm worried about you. That's why I'm telling you all this. I'm afraid if you get too close you're going to get hurt."

"If this guy is really from Chicago, he's probably connected to a bootlegging gang. Crossing state lines makes this a federal issue. If I can prove that—"

"I *can't* be your proof. There's too much at stake for me, my family, and the people I distribute for."

"I know. I'll find another way." I reached over the table and smoothed his wild lock of hair.

Walter swallowed hard. "I've got to get word to my employers, but I can't do it over the phone. I'm leaving tonight, and I probably won't be back for a while."

"Let's get you out of here."

Walter was scared and rightly so. If the guy he led to the store was the killer, Walter was also in danger.

Nathan let us out and quickly latched the door. A cloud of cigarette smoke came with us.

We hadn't walked three feet from the back door when a man approached us from across the alley.

"Shit, Elsie," Walter spoke through clenched teeth. He thrust his arm out in front of me and we stopped.

The man tapped the brim of his hat and spoke, his harsh voice clashing with his attempt at polite conversation. "Evening. I've been looking for you."

Walter whispered to me. "You go on ahead. I'll meet you."

Keeping my eyes on the suspect, I didn't move. It was hard to make out many details in the dark alley, but enough light came from the windows for me to match the man standing in front of me to Walter's description. His hand was thrust in the side pocket of his overcoat.

"I heard what happened to those shopkeepers the other night, and while I'm sorry about it, I'm still in need of what I came here for. I was hoping you could help me out."

"If you think I'm going to help you after . . ." Walter couldn't bring himself to finish.

The man's eyebrows came together in the center and he raised his hands in the air. "You don't think I had anything to do with that, do you?"

"You were the last person there that night," Walter said. The contempt in his tone was thick.

"Do I look like I need money?"

"The papers might be calling it a robbery, but I know better."

"Now, you've got it all wrong. I'm just here to do a little business." Arms held away from his sides, he advanced several steps. "I just need to speak to the people who are making what you're delivering."

Planting his legs wider, Walter said, "I don't know where it comes from."

"I doubt that. Tell me what you know."

"That's not going to happen."

"Not a wise move, kid." His eyes turned hard and cold.

"The trail stopped with Mr. Brownfield. I can't tell you a damn thing."

"You want to end up like him?"

"You can't get anything from me if I'm dead."

"That's true." The man pulled a gun from his coat and pointed it at me. "Looks to me like I have another option."

Walter balled up each of his fists and stood in front of me.

The man's lips drew back, revealing the whites of his teeth. "Noble kid," he sneered, "but you don't seem to understand."

At that point, Mave's back door swung open and a young couple came laughing out the door, illuminating us with a brief bright light. They were drunk and teasing each other and paid us no mind whatsoever, heading in the opposite direction. Nathan locked the door behind them and didn't notice us, either. We all stayed silent until the couple was around the corner.

"As I was saying—" the man began, but his words were abruptly halted as something plunged down and broke apart on top of his head. The gun went off and Walter cried out.

The man slumped to the ground. Fine grains and hard pieces of what seemed like stone collected at our feet.

"What in the hell just happened?" Walter asked.

The man was unconscious, so I grabbed his gun and placed it inside my coat pocket.

Nathan pulled aside the peephole and shouted out, "What the hell is going on out there?" Assured that the law or any other trouble wasn't on the other side of the door, he yanked it open, illuminating ceramic pieces all over the ground, a significant amount of dirt, and a now homeless plant.

I looked up past Nathan into an open second-floor window where Louise stood peering at us from a lighted room. Her loose blond hair hung down around her face.

"That's not a nice man, Miss Elsie."

"No, Louise. He most definitely is not."

"That was a good thing I did."

"It certainly was and I thank you." I pulled handcuffs from my coat and fastened them around Barzetti's wrists. "That'll hold him until the sheriff arrives. Nate, please get Mave. She'll need to know about this."

"Will do. Walter, are you okay?"

A sheen of white had broken out over Walter's face, and he seemed to sway a little on his feet while grasping his upper arm.

"Walter?" I pulled his coat aside. Even in the half-light, I saw the dark stain blooming through his shirt.

He grimaced. "It's just my arm. I'll live."

"We've still got to get you help, Walter." I pulled a handkerchief from my coat and tied it around his arm to stop the flow of blood.

"I'm fine, really."

I wasn't convinced, but shortly after that, Mave came out. I explained what was going on, and she agreed that despite the hassle, it was altogether necessary to call the authorities. The man who most likely murdered the Brownfields was caught. That was the important thing. All agreed that the truth was best in this case, most of the truth anyway.

Walter quietly insisted that he be kept out of it, still wanting to appear clean of involvement with liquor. The local police accepted regular bribes to look the other way, but no one knew what the new sheriff's views about liquor were yet. Most importantly, Walter needed to stay clear of the gang. He knew too much. He rested in a side room at Mave's and waited for me to be done with the sheriff.

Though Barzetti was handcuffed and still seemingly knocked out, Nathan stood with a lamp in hand, his foot pressing down on the man's back. I reached into his pockets, found a wallet, and pulled out an outdated military identification card that read, "Tino Cerone, Private First

Class." That wasn't the name he had given Walter, but no surprise there.

A sheriff's department auto pulled into the alley, and I was surprised to see only one deputy emerge from the vehicle. It was the same young face I had seen on the Brownfield's porch on Saturday. "There better be more of you coming," I warned.

"The sheriff and the others were called out."

"This man is dangerous, probably connected to Chicago gang activity, and the primary suspect in the murders of Homer and Rosela Brownfield. You should've brought backup."

"Doesn't look too dangerous to me." He kicked at Cerone's shoe. "Passed out flat. Handcuffed. Unarmed now, I assume?"

"He is. Here's his gun. Enter it as evidence. It's likely the same weapon used to murder the couple on the Lincoln Highway."

"That right?"

"As you saw, he's handcuffed. Here are the keys. I'll pick them up when I come in to make my statement."

I wanted to be present for the suspect's questioning, but it was more important to take Walter to safety first and get him some medical attention. We had no way of knowing whether there were more gang members on the way. With the rest of the sheriff's department out on another call, it was likely Barzetti or Cerone, whatever his name was, wouldn't be questioned until the next day, anyway. That whole thing could sit and stew. Walter needed my help.

I met Fedelma, a local mystic whose herbal healing methods were widely known, at the county fair eleven years ago. "He won't be the best in the game anymore," she had

predicted, just hours before a celebrated pilot, Louis Rosenbaum, crashed to his death. As far as I knew, I was the only one still alive who had heard that strange prophecy.

Many years later I saw her again. She lived near the Wapsipinicon River, down a poorly maintained county road. An investigation brought Phinny and me there as we searched for the body of young Cleveland Mattheisen. Fedelma led us to his decayed corpse wedged just under the roots of a fallen tree along the riverbank. Cleveland wasn't the victim of foul play at all, just the victim of his own bad judgment when he decided to swim in the unpredictable spring waters.

I had no idea how Fedelma knew he was there, for he wasn't visible from any place she could likely reach with her elderly frame, but she pointed the way nonetheless.

Fedelma worked as a seer and healer, receiving payment in trade. Locals visited her cabin for visions of the future. She provided those visions in the form of symbolic paintings she did not explain fully, and for healing, both physical and mental.

Curious, I visited Fedelma on a whim one summer day. She made her herbal tea and hovered her gnarled hands over my body while chanting Old German phrases meant to calm and soothe a troubled soul.

Her angles on life soon became a haven for me in my unpredictable world. I trusted her and sat at her table many afternoons, even when feeling fine. I watched her take care of a hunter who had been peppered with birdshot and a boy who had caught his own foot in a trap instead of the bobcat he intended.

Fedelma smelled of thyme and sage, the earth. She pulled all manner of natural things from the myriad pockets in her skirt and jacket, had herbs down in her boots.

On a small table in a corner of her cabin sat her paints and brushes. Hanging above it were paintings she made for herself and paintings left behind by people who didn't want to accept what she had to tell.

My mother told me there were many women like Fedelma who brought knowledge with them from the Old Country. It seemed like magic, but really it wasn't magic at all. It was an ancient knowledge of herbs and intentions, observation and intuition, a sixth sense of knowing that was no more unusual than any other wonder of nature.

So that's why I took Walter to Fedelma instead of to the hospital. Walter needed to drop off the known world for a while. Fedelma had no telephone and no neighbors.

She was dressed in her nightclothes, a long nightgown and heavy robe, and her long gray hair was out of its bun. "I felt you coming," she said.

"He's shot."

"Of course he is." Turning to Walter she said, "Get yourself to the bed."

Fedelma's cabin was simple and practical. One big room served as kitchen, sitting room, library, and bedroom all in one. There were no decorations of any kind; every item had a purpose. The drying herbs that hung from the rafters were beautiful enough, and the crystals and gems that lined the windowsills shed an aura of peace.

"Start some water boiling. Fill the kettle to the top." Fedelma motioned me toward the stove, then unwrapped Walter's bandage, carefully removed his shirt, and felt the back and sides of his arm. A small dark hole bored into his triceps, but a larger hole twice as big mangled the back of his arm. She clicked her tongue. "Lucky for you it's not stuck in there and luckier still you can move the arm. That means nothing major was hit—no bone, no artery, just muscle and nerves—all of which can grow back themselves. It's likely there are bits of your shirt in there. We need to wash those out."

When the water was ready, Fedelma poured some of it into a shallow basin. Snatching several sprigs of herb from a jar she said, "I'll wash my hands in this water before tending to you. It's infused with rosemary and has healing power in it." She emptied more water into a quart jar and added a pinch of salt and several drops of lavender oil. Its aroma filled my nose and reminded me of Rosela Brownfield's autopsy. "This solution will clean the wound."

She told Walter to lie down and handed me an empty basin. "Place this underneath the arm."

Mumbling something under her breath, Fedelma fished out the rosemary springs from the basin and washed her hands in the water. She turned to Walter with the jar of lavender. "It's time to cleanse the wound. You'll have to lie still. Elsie, hold the arm."

I sat at the foot of the bed and grasped Walter's elbow, pressing it down as firmly as I dared.

Walter turned his face to the wall. He flinched slightly but didn't make a sound as the cleansing solution began to do its job.

The mixture trickled slowly over his arm and Fedelma chanted over and over again in German, "May the natural way be with you."

After it had dried, she tied a bandage firmly around the wound. "Now go to sleep. You'll need rest for it to heal, and I've no interest in seeing you lose that arm. You won't leave until morning."

Neither of us bothered to protest.

With an ancient set of cards, Fedelma played solitaire into the night. At least I think that's what it was. The light from her lamp played off our skin as we fell asleep.

Tino Cerone

When The Vulture died, I walked into the war office and signed up for the army. The Great War was raging, and while I had a job, I didn't have a home anymore. All I had to do was lie about my age a little and they shipped me off to St. Nazaire, France, where I fought Germans with the first infantry division.

That was a mistake. Street life is hard, but war is harder.

Won't tell you a damn thing about the war, but I'll tell you something about getting there.

All kinds of guys join the army. Some of them, like me, aren't so nice. My bunkmate couldn't stand me on account of the fact that I'm Italian. The feeling was mutual. The stronzo said one slur too many and he found himself floating in the Atlantic. A casualty of war.

I slugged him a good one. He lost his balance, gripped the side, and I helped gravity a little. A small tip and he was gone, just like that.

That's not the story, though. It's what happened after I pitched him over.

82

Someone spotted him in the water, yelled, "Man overboard, man overboard!" Horns sounded, all hands on deck.

That was a sight. A thousand men running from above and below to see him floating, flailing, drowning.

A thousand men have the power to move ships, and that's what they did. They ran to the starboard side, causing the ship to list so badly I swear I could have dipped my hand right in the water. Maybe it didn't tip that far, but far enough to lose my footing and to imagine what it would be like to float in the cold Atlantic. To die there with the fishes.

I can swim well enough, but hell, if you don't die from drowning, there's a hundred other things that can snuff you out. It's just a matter of time. First off, the Atlantic is cold. Like as not, you'll die from the shock of it. Hypothermia, they call it. You'll float there for a couple hours, gradually losing your ability to think, to move. Then you lose consciousness. The end.

If you're in a spot that's not so cold, a warm current say, then next up is dehydration. The shit of it. You're surrounded by water, but can't drink a drop of the stuff. If you do, you'll vomit until your insides come out and go crazy. Again, the end.

Sunburn.

Jellyfish stings.

Storms.

Rogue waves.

No food.

Sharks.

Anything I don't see coming scares the hell out of me. I want to know my end is near, you know? The vastness of the ocean deep underneath you, the endless sea of predators looking for food, and there you are—a little bobber just floating, just waiting to be eaten.

After the tip, nobody cared about saving one dying man. They all wanted to save themselves. Back up! Port side! Port side! By the time the ship was righted, the guy was gone. Drowned or maybe floating behind us somewhere and watching, terrified, as we sailed away.

Eventually, he was fish food, but the funny thing is, he was a lucky bastard to have died however he did.

The rest of us moved on to a horror far worse. I guarantee it.

If I had to do it all over again, I'd have let him live.

Elsie Edens
Tuesday, November 7, 1922

Magic . . . is the ancient and absolute science of nature and her laws.
—A.L. Constant

Long before sunrise, Fedelma's voice reached into my consciousness and surrounded me with a soft green light. For a time, I bathed in it, felt the illumination trickle between my fingers and fill my ears. I realized as I woke that Fedelma's voice surrounded the cabin. Curious, I peered through a greasy window and saw Fedelma walking counterclockwise, holding a lantern in one hand and a palm-sized green sphere in the other. Her long gray hair floated in a soft wind. I watched and listened for several minutes. If Fedelma was aware of me spying, she showed no sign of it.

When she came inside, Fedelma brought the scent of river winds with her. She set down her lantern and put the green sphere inside a cloth-lined box. I handed her a cup of coffee, and she motioned for me to come outside. Leaving a still-sleeping Walter, we went out to the porch despite the bitter chill and sat on two weathered wooden chairs.

"You're up against something that can take the both of you. You'll need to be smart, and you'll need to listen to me."

"I trust you. That's why I'm here."

"Go with him. Stay there for as long as you can. Honey lures like a trap. Use it."

"I . . . I have no idea what that means."

"You will, when the time comes." She fished around inside her skirt pocket and pulled out a pointed green crystal hanging from a brown leather cord. "Take this."

"What is it?"

"Jasper. It has my intention with it. It will protect you as much as it can."

I placed it around my neck and tucked it inside my shirt.

"I'll prepare things for you to take, things to care for the wound. You saw what I did last night. I'll show you again before you go. You'll do that every night until the wound is closed. Don't fail in this, no matter what happens. Infection could cause the loss of the arm. If thick pus that's green or yellow comes from it, get to a hospital."

The smell of bacon and eggs woke Walter from his heavy slumber. After a second cleansing, Fedelma fashioned him a simple sling to keep his arm still, and we ate a quiet breakfast.

When it was time to go, Walter thanked Fedelma, and she tucked a small brown satchel in his jacket.

Walter grimaced. "I don't need to see it to know what that is. What's the garlic for?"

"Crush and eat a clove a day or steep it in hot water; let Elsie tend to you each night. As long as your wound stays clean, you'll have no trouble from it."

Walter thanked her again.

"No need for more thanks," Fedelma said. "Just do as I told you. That's the best kind of gratitude."

She gave me a bag filled with rosemary, lavender oil, and salt. "By the time these are gone, the wound should be closed up."

In the car, I turned to Walter. "Where do you want to go?"

"Head north. We're going to Hurstville."

The town of Hurstville was a sixty-minute drive on a good day. As long as the rain held off, the way was clear enough. Walter didn't complain about the bumpy ride, but he gritted his teeth and held on to the dash with his good arm. I tried my best to navigate around the holes in the dirt road, but I could only do so much.

When we passed into Jackson County, a western wall of darkening clouds smashed into what had already been hanging in the atmosphere, shrouding any possible light from the rising sun. Thunder rumbled its warning.

It started with heavy drops, slow and teasing. With each impact, tiny plumes of road dust lifted.

I asked Walter, "Did it ever occur to you that you might find good work on the legal side of things?"

"I tried that."

"You're . . . how old are you? You can't be any older than—"

"Eighteen."

"You can't have looked for honest work for long, if you're only eighteen."

"That's . . . I'm not in the mood for this right now."

The rain picked up into a predictable cadence, softening the road and forcing me to slow my speed considerably.

"You have to wonder what things would be like for you otherwise."

"But this isn't *otherwise*, Elsie. It's what it is, and I can't do anything to turn that around now."

As if to accentuate his point, or, perhaps, to refute it, a crack of lightning shot down in the western sky, then another, and another.

I recalled my own failures in judgment, of which there were many, but instead of shutting me up, my recollections only fueled my antagonism.

"What now, Walter? Where is this going to lead?"

"I told you, we're going to Hurstville."

"For God's sake, don't be dense."

We passed through Maquoketa, its streets quiet except for the downpour descending all around. It was too early for the stores and shops to be open for the day, so we drove through undetected.

"Should we stop here?" I asked as we reached the opposite edge of town, unsure of the likelihood of further progress. The muddy roads were only getting worse, and the sky showed no signs of letting go of the blanket of rain it had drawn over us.

"We have to keep going."

"Are you sure? I can't get stuck, Walter. I have business back home." I wanted to get Walter to safety, but I needed to find a way to balance that with the ability to get back to Clinton. I still needed to speak to Phinny about the night's events. Rosela's sister deserved an update. The Clinton County Sheriff's Department surely expected a statement from me sooner rather than later, but I hadn't yet worked out exactly what I would say. "There's no way for you to—"

"Will you just keep driving?" He accentuated the last three words slowly, eyes closed.

Both hands on the wheel, leaning toward the dash, I drove on.

Two miles from our destination, the vehicle lost hold of the road, carried by rivulets of mud. I moved the wheel this way and that, but there was no controlling it. We braced ourselves against the odd angle and slid smoothly, like a pat of butter racing down a warm ear of corn, headfirst into the ditch. The splash sent a cannonball of water in every direction. We sat quiet for a few seconds, disbelief at the situation shutting us up for a little while. Unfortunately, the ditch was steep enough to eliminate all possibility of extraction without the aid of a truck to yank my car out.

"There goes the other headlight," I said. First the deer, and now this, I thought. My poor auto had been through the wringer.

"You're a hell of a driver."

Though I knew Walter meant it lightheartedly, his comment only made me angry.

I held both arms out straight to keep from sliding into the wheel. "I knew this was going to happen."

Walter adjusted the sling on his arm and rested his back against the dash.

"Now what?" I hollered at him.

"Now we walk."

"That's just great."

"I can't do anything to turn things around now, least of all this car. You drove us into a steep and muddy ditch."

"Thank you for stating the obvious."

"My pleasure."

Though madder than a wet hen, I helped Walter up the steep embankment as best I could. My best wasn't very sturdy considering the circumstances, and I lost my footing, resulting in an unladylike sprawl face down in the rain-drenched ditch. Somehow, Walter managed to climb to the top and looked down on my prone figure. My chin rested on a deepening puddle while the entirety of the rest of me lay in it, fingers buried in mud.

Walter made a lame attempt at stifling a laugh and turned his back on me. His shoulders shook with laughter.

Other than his wet clothing, he was unscathed. I couldn't possibly let that rest, so as I stumbled up, I grabbed a handful of mud and while his back was still turned, slung it right at him. The amorphous blob hit the bottom half of his head and upper back, making its point. It was my turn to laugh, and laugh I did, letting out a snort along with it. Embarrassed, I brought my hand up to my nose and smeared it with more mud.

Walter lowered his head and peeked at me over his shoulder, making sure I wasn't ready with another volley of ammunition. Sure I was too taken with laughter to manage another successful strike, he turned with a grin and held his hand out for me.

Every inch of us was soaked through by the time we managed to stumble into Hurstville. The only good thing about the rain was it washed away any mud that clung to my face and torso, so instead of looking like a barnyard pig, I just looked like a drowned rat with dirty feet. The still ravaging downpour blurred the lights emerging from shop windows and homes, so that their promise of dry warmth seemed more like a dream than reality.

The town nestled at the base of a limestone bluff. Just before its center, along the left side of the road, were twelve whitewashed homes, chipped and ruddy with age. Each had its own small barn and outhouse. Lamp light flickered from within, revealing mothers bustling to get children ready for school and fathers dressing for work. On the last porch, a grandfather smoking a pipe rocked in a wooden chair. Walter waved at him, resulting in a slow disbelieving wave in return. *Am I really seeing you out there in this rain? Why don't you have an auto? Or an umbrella? Are you mad?*

A hundred yards beyond, numerous buildings hugged the only public road in town—large barns and sheds, a general store and café, a post office, and the typical odds and ends of a small country town. On the east side of the road, against the cliff itself and running up its 30-foot height, were four six-foot wide smokestacks, and at the base of each, long sheds in need of renovation. The corner of one was patched together with a mismatch of wood and shingles, the victim of a fallen tree or wayward vehicle, perhaps. A wooden unloading platform ran the length of the cliff behind the iron tops of the stacks. I had heard of the Hurstville lime business before but wasn't altogether clear on what the chimneys were for.

Shouting over the deluge, Walter pointed at the café. "You can get hot coffee there. I'll be right back. I know someone who might be able to get your car out." Before I could utter any kind of protest, he tramped off behind the buildings and disappeared.

While the sign prominently displayed "OPEN," the door seemed to be stuck. Frustrated, I shoved too hard and nearly sprawled for the second time that morning as I burst into the place, slipping on my own wetness as it pooled underneath me.

A voice called from the back of the store, "What's the ruckus out there? Better not be you, Cornelius, dripping your manure-soaked boots all over my clean floor!" A woman emerged, wiping her hands on her apron. She was about forty, thick in the middle, and pretty, with long brown hair and shining grey eyes that softened as soon as she saw me. "Oh, my, Miss, you're soaked through!" She grabbed a towel from a shelf behind the counter and tossed it to me. "You're not from here. Did you have an accident?"

"I, we did. We ran off the road just there." I pointed in the general direction of where I thought my car was, though admittedly I was turned around altogether, the rain and drama of it all dulling my sense of direction.

"Put that towel underneath you. You've a river of rain heading right into the floorboards." She tossed me another towel. "Dry yourself with that one."

"I'm so sorry."

"Heavens, it's nothing to be sorry for. You can't help it. I suppose I'm a bit of a crank about my floors. It's a losing

91

battle around here, with the cattle manure and lime dust coating everything. The men don't pay it a bit of mind. Just waltz in and expect me to clean up after them. Today'll be a day of mud on top of it."

"May I use your phone?" I wanted to call Phinny and Mama immediately. "I can pay."

"Sure, but it won't do you a bit of good now. Phones are out. Storm downed some lines somewhere. One of these days, they'll figure out how to make the system more reliable."

No phone service, continually degrading roads, it was a pickle all right.

Phinny and Mama would worry about me and what I was up to, but as long as the suspect was behind bars, the sheriff could wait. I decided I needed to talk to Phinny before discussing anything with the sheriff. He would understand about Walter. He would help me figure out what to say.

The woman handed me a cup of coffee, and I sipped it while waiting for Walter to find me.

I was on my second cup by the time Walter poked his head in the door, reluctant to come inside. He clearly knew the woman, for he called to her. "Alice?"

The woman came from the back. "Walter! Are you with this poor woman?"

"I am."

"For heaven's sake, find her some warm, dry clothes."

"Taking care of that. Don't you worry." Walter winked at her. A gesture I had never seen him make, and I puzzled over his familiarity. "I've a favor to ask of you first."

"What is it this time?"

"Just please don't mention you saw me and a beautiful young lady come through here, okay?"

Beautiful? I thought. Does he mean me? I had never considered myself anything remotely close to beautiful, and even if I was, I was sure my sodden state had washed any traces of it away.

Alice agreed. "You don't have to worry about me saying a thing."

Walter took me to a large shed that sat alongside the rail yards. Next to it was a long barn. Many cattle shuffled and lowed inside. It reminded me of my sister's Elvira farm, and I felt a twinge of nostalgia.

As soon as we ran in, a colored man in overalls hauled the sliding doors shut behind us. He had strangely protruding ears emphasized by his close-cropped black hair. Without pause for greeting, he walked to a room in the back, returning with another man who was middle-aged and well-dressed.

"Welcome, Miss Edens. I'm Stanley Kaufman." As he approached, he rolled up each shirtsleeve and motioned toward the other man. "This is Marcus."

Marcus was slightly stooped and looked at the floor while hooking his thumbs in the straps of his overalls. I was surprised to see a colored man in such a small Iowa town.

Stanley continued, "Thank you for bringing Walter to us. And I'm sorry about your car, though not sure when we'll be able to get you out. We'll need some dry ground first, and that doesn't look likely any time soon."

"I really have to get back. Is there any way?"

"Not unless you can fly, miss. Or swim like a fish. No one'll be on the roads today." Stanley didn't give me a chance to protest further. He turned to Marcus and instructed, "Get them to Helen's. They can get dry up there. I'll take care of getting the auto covered in case prying eyes make it up our way. Tell my brother to meet us there. I want them both to hear what these two have to say."

93

Marcus led Walter and me up a long set of limestone stairs; they wrapped around the right side of the bluff and away from the center of the company town. He held a dark umbrella over my head though I assured him it wasn't necessary; I was already soaking wet. I peered through bare trees at the row of houses we passed on the way in.

Marcus followed my gaze. "The men who live there used to work fulltime blasting lime in the quarries, feeding the chimneys, and preparing shipments."

"Used to?"

"The lime business is nearly bust."

"What do they do now?"

"A variety of things. We do occasionally get an order for lime, so it's not all said and done, but some of the men have found work in Maquoketa, some are farm hands, some do other things. The women work in the stores here and take care of the little ones."

"What is the lime business, exactly?"

Marcus hitched the thumb of his free hand underneath the strap of his overalls. "Builders use powdered limestone in mortar."

"How does it go from rock to powder?"

"We start by blasting rock in the quarries around here. Lots of them due to the Maquoketa River that runs just a half mile or so that way." He nodded his chin in front of us to the east, toward a deep stand of trees. "In the quarries, limestone is broken up into smaller hunks of rock that are carried to carts and hauled by mules to the tops of the four kilns. The furnaces break limestone down into fine powder by driving out the water. At the base of each kiln, men shovel the lime onto rock slabs inside the cooling sheds. When ready, the cooled lime is packed into barrels and shipped by rail."

"And who is Helen?" I asked.

"Mr. Kaufman's sister," Walter said. He trudged up the stairs behind us. I wondered about his arm.

"She and Mr. Kaufman each have a house to themselves. Neither one married. Those houses there," Marcus pointed at six more small homes that ran through the sloping timber to our right, "used to be all occupied, but they're almost all empty now. All but one. I live at that one on the end, closest to us."

At the top of the hill, the stairs met a fifty-yard lane of limestone gravel reaching toward two grand white farmhouses alike in every way except only one had lights burning inside. Each had a three-sided wraparound porch and a cupola built into the roof.

A row of towering white pines hugged the left side of the lane, but they did nothing to block the onslaught of rain that funneled down on us in great pine-scented droplets.

Fall mums of various red and purple hues lined the sides of the road, a backdrop to the myriad of once-flowering summer plants before them, most of which were beaten down by the rain. The immense flower beds were free of weeds, clearly loved by someone with great skill and patience.

To the right of the main houses, an acre of wildflowers served as the home to twelve white bee boxes of various heights. Around each one, the tall grass was close-trimmed.

"Here we are," said Marcus. "Just don't say much and you'll be fine. Helen can be a little jumpy, and just so you know, she always carries a gun in her apron."

Walter smirked and caught my eye.

Marcus knocked on the wooden door, looked back at us with an assuring grin, and ran his hand around his waistline to make sure his shirt was tucked in.

A tall, lanky woman in her forties yanked open the door and peered out at us through fogged glasses. "Who's with you? I can't see a damn thing through the steam from the oven." The woman pulled off her glasses and squinted.

"This is Walter; you know him—and his lady friend, Elsie Edens. Mr. Kaufman sent us."

"Get on in here then." Helen cleaned her glasses with a hand towel. The front of her apron was dusted with flour. While inspecting the lenses, Helen backed up into the kitchen, allowing us to step inside. "And what am I to do with you?"

"We were hoping for some dry clothes. Our car ran off the road," Walter said.

"You're fools to be out in this rain. Serves you right."

Walter pulled his wet shirt away from his chest. "We have some news that couldn't wait."

"I suppose I'll get you those dry clothes, so I can hear it. I'll start with you." Helen looked me up and down, then went upstairs.

"Don't take Helen's abruptness personally. She's like that with everybody," Marcus whispered.

When she returned, Helen pointed me to the washroom just off the kitchen and handed me a bundle of clothes. "You can clean up in there and leave your wet things in the tub."

A slow drip came from the sink in the washroom, leaving a rusty ring in the bowl. On the wall above the tub was a painting of a single bee, its parts labeled with calligraphic ink: Thorax, compound eye, abdomen, forewing, hindwing, pollen press, stinger.

I undressed quietly, so as to hear the conversation through the door.

"Mr. Kaufman wants me to fetch your brother and bring him here, too," Marcus said to Helen.

"Get on with it then. I've got plenty I need to do today."

I peered out through the skeleton keyhole and watched as Helen walked Marcus to the door. His hand lingered on her elbow for a split second before he went back out into the rain.

I continued to watch, curious about how well Walter knew the woman.

"What happened to you?" Helen asked.

"We ran off the road."

"I know that part. Why's your arm in a sling?"

"I was shot."

Helen approached him, her right hand touching the pocket of her apron. "Who shot you?"

"It's a long story, but that's why we're here."

"Is it bad?"

"Nah, just a scratch, really. Nothing to worry about. Do you mind if I smoke in here?" Walter held up a cigarette.

"I do mind. Won't have that nasty stuff in my house. You'll live without it."

Walter offered no protest.

I was relieved to be dry and warm but felt awkward in Helen's clothes. Thankfully, the floor-length skirt she gave me had two long pockets—plenty of room for my knife and the assorted tools and notebooks I normally kept in my long coat. I stepped out into the kitchen feeling like an actress in a play. As I smoothed the skirt, Walter smirked at me.

"Thank you for the warm things," I said to Helen.

"Somehow they don't look your style," Helen said.

"I'd rather wear pants these days."

"Is that right?" Helen smiled. She stuck a leg out from behind her apron and showed off her own brown pants. "I'd give you my pair, but I've got them on." Grabbing an umbrella from a stand near the door, she left to find Walter some clothes at her brother's house.

"Why did you want to come here, Walter?" I said, turning to face him.

He rose and stood over by the open oven door warming himself while adjusting his sling. A pan of warm biscuits cooled on the counter. "Helen, Stanley, and their brother, Bernard, run the business in Hurstville. They bought it from Alfred and William Hurst. You've heard of them?"

I had. The Hurst brothers were regionally famous for their entrepreneurship, having started the lime business themselves, establishing a company-owned and self-sustaining town. All adult residents had worked for the Hursts, who were known to provide fair wages and treat their employees like family.

"Before the Kaufmans took over, this place did pretty well for itself."

"Before?"

"It wasn't their fault, just bad luck."

"What happened?" The scent of those biscuits had my mouth watering.

"Bad timing is all. I think it was 1915. Alfred Hurst passed away and William Hurst decided to sell the business. The Kaufmans had researched the success of the place and decided to spend their inheritance on the venture. What they didn't know was that just a year before they bought the company, Portland Cement came out on the market and began edging out the demand for lime. By 1920, they never had reason to fire all four kilns again and had to lay off many of the workers. They had no choice."

"How do they make a go of it?"

"They've found a way to keep things afloat."

"How? And how do you know these people? Why are we here?"

"The Kaufmans have another business, Elsie. They make the best honey-flavored whiskey in the Midwest. That's why we're in trouble."

Hurstville was a curious place, no doubt. I never saw it in its heyday, but at one time the town had indeed thrived.

Before the lime business slowed, the fire and brimstone furnaces had denuded the countryside for three decades, belching black smoke into the air seven months a year. Massive amounts of cordwood were consumed in order to eliminate moisture from the stone and break it down into powder. The two Hurst brothers, Alfred and William, had owned more than 700 acres of land, and for a time, the forests there were sufficient. In the coldest months, temperatures didn't allow the furnaces to burn hot enough, so the Hurstville community earned a living by cutting lumber instead. The success of the limestone business, however, required even more trees than their own land could provide, so farmers began selling lumber to the company. A wood crisis eventually developed, as the county was nearly stripped of all its trees.

That was the Jackson County the Kaufmans moved in to. Though the arrival of Portland Cement was not good for the lime business, it was good for the land. The countryside breathed a sigh of relief and began to clothe herself slowly, like a shy bride, reforesting along riverbanks and other out of the way places with oaks and linden, sugar maple, dogwood and serviceberry—a complete wardrobe.

Though the Kaufmans took over at an unfortunate time, another opportunity did present itself.

Some states enacted their own form of Prohibition before the Eighteenth Amendment affected all of them in 1920. The Eighteenth banned alcohol production, distribution, and sale, maintaining a citizen's right to consume and possess alcohol produced before the ban. Since Iowa began looking at temperance laws in 1847 and enforced statewide Prohibition in earnest in 1916, Iowa's inhabitants were ahead of the curve when it came to the acquisition of spirits.

Where there's demand, supply follows. Local distillers took care of the local population, and they all learned to blend in like camouflage.

Instead of harvesting trees and lime, the Kaufmans turned to an annual crop for profit. Templeton, Iowa, had its rye, but all of Iowa had corn. A major ingredient in moonshine whiskey, corn grew there in some of the richest soil one could hope to come by.

The other thing Iowa had was a heavily rural environment, perfect for discretion. Farmers made moonshine in caves, hog sheds, and duck blinds. Even Benedictine brothers tended secluded vineyards and bottled wine sanctioned only because of its religious applications. The sympathetic church sold countless bottles to thirsty parishioners. German families, reluctant to give up a liquid lifeline to the homeland, made home brew beer by the barrel.

For the Kaufmans, turning to whiskey production was a natural transition. The English immigrants, Bernard and Stanley, were taught the trade by their father who had been too prone to drinking to survive past middle age. While Stanley didn't carry on the tradition of home distillation, Bernard certainly did. Long before the impending demise of the lime business worried the Kaufmans, Bernard maintained his own private still across the river. When the idea to expand Bernard's hobby into a business was proposed by Helen in order to supplement their income, both brothers jumped at the idea. Bernard had several copper stills fashioned in the blacksmith shop under his careful supervision. The unused barrels that had been solely intended to ship lime were now used to age the whiskey Bernard distilled. They were also used as a convenient disguise for the shipment of their whiskey by rail. The Kaufmans had everything they needed to make a go of it.

Five of us gathered in Helen's kitchen. She and Stanley sat at the ends of the table with Walter, Marcus, and me taking the sides.

Helen served plates of biscuits and gravy, and Marcus poured coffee, as a grizzled-looking man with unkempt salt-and-pepper hair and matching beard let himself in the door. The sharp scent of the distillery trailed off his work clothes. Sitting down he said, "What's this about?"

"First things first, brother," Stanley said. "This is Elsie Edens, a friend of Walter's. She's working as a private investigator and looking into the deaths of Homer and Rosela Brownfield."

Helen set a plate in front of Bernard.

"And what does that have to do with us?" Bernard asked.

"None of you are suspects, of course," I said.

"Of course." Bernard avoided my gaze, his mouth full.

"The papers reported it was a robbery," Helen said.

"The papers are wrong," I explained. "We have good reason to believe a Chicago gang is responsible." I grabbed hold of the jasper necklace Fedelma had given me and rubbed my thumb over its smooth surface.

"What makes you think that?" Stanley asked.

Walter informed them of his first discussion with Tino Cerone in the alley, how he led him to the Brownfield store, and what happened after our discussion at Mave's the night before. He did not tell them that he had taken the whiskey from the store basement, however. That bit he kept to himself.

Helen asked, "If the Chicago gang wants to buy from us, why would they have killed the Brownfields? That doesn't make sense."

"There's no doubt some things don't add up," I said, "but they are looking for you, and if they really want to, sooner or later they're going to find you. You need to have a plan when they do."

"That planning's best done in closer company." Bernard looked at me through his long hair.

Walter spoke with his mouth full. "Elsie can keep secrets better than anyone I know."

"That right?" Bernard asked.

"I'm a private investigator, Mr. Kaufman. I've no special fondness for Prohibition, so your business is safe. My job, as I was hired to do by Rosela's sister, was to find out who killed the Brownfields and bring him to justice. That man is now behind bars, but I don't think it ends there. That's why we're here. If a Chicago gang is on the way, none of you are safe."

Bernard pushed his empty plate away and took a gulp of coffee.

Stanley said, "Prohibition is giving more strength to city gangs. Wouldn't be at all surprised if they start organizing and reaching beyond city borders."

"What would they want with us?" Helen asked.

For a moment, everyone at the table kept their thoughts to themselves, then Stanley broke the silence. "They're trying to shut us down."

Bernard said, "Why would some Chicago gang care about what we're doing in Iowa?"

"Alcohol is where the real money is now, and they want to be the ones who provide it," Stanley explained.

Helen nodded and said, "It'll be at least a couple of days before the roads are passable. Likely as long until the phones are working again. We have that much time to develop a plan."

"Quitting isn't an option," Bernard said. "I won't do that."

"I need some time to think," Stanley said. He looked at Bernard and Helen in turn. "We have a hard decision to make."

I spent that night at Helen's while Walter slept at Stanley's house just across the lawn. I had tried using Helen's phone numerous times that afternoon to no avail, so was awake and worried about what Mama and Phinny must be thinking. Insomnia set in so thoroughly, the more I tried to calm myself to sleep, the more my mind raced. In my teen years, I suffered from chronic bouts of insomnia. Mama placed sprigs of lavender inside my pillowcase and taught me to focus on my breath moving in and out like the ocean tides. Sometimes it worked, sometimes it didn't. That night I gave up when the waxing moon poked through the dispersing clouds and shone through the lace curtains onto my bed. I wrapped a honeybee-patterned quilt around my shoulders and sat on an old wooden chair at the window. Looking up at the moon, Walter stood smoking a cigarette in the light of Stanley's porch lamp. It wasn't until I saw him shifting the sling that I remembered Fedelma's directions to care for the wound each night. With a start, I gathered the care package of herbs, salt, and clean bandages and headed downstairs.

I fetched Walter from Stanley's porch and brought him into Helen's kitchen where I had started a pot of boiling water. The evening was balmy for November, but Walter shivered as he took off the sling and his shirt. A ring of red flared around the wound and the skin around it had purpled slightly, but there was no sign of infection.

After the water had cooled, I instructed him to hold his arm over the tub in the adjoining bathroom. While I poured the water over his wound, I noticed that he smelled of garlic; he had taken Fedelma's advice and had eaten the bulbs she gave him to ward off infection.

"This whole thing has me pretty shook up," Walter said.

"It has me shook up, too, Walter. We'd be fools not to be scared."

"You know," Walter said, grimacing, "my greatest fear used to be that I'd turn into my father."

"You're nothing like him. Why would you be worried about that?" I had finished pouring the water on his arm, but Walter kept it over the tub while the last rivulets ran down the drain.

"Sure he had a temper and a tendency for violence," Walter said, "but he could also be the most charming man in town if he felt like it. Most people were completely fooled by him. 'Bet you want to be just like your Pa,' they told me, and sometimes, I did. When he was in a good mood, he would take me to the tobacco store in Plugtown. Men gathered there to share stories and gossip. I sat on a rickety wooden chair, listening closely to everything the men had to say. I watched Pa take over the room with his lively stories. He'd jive and bounce and wave his arms, and tell funny tales he never told at home. The men laughed, and I did, too. I wondered if those men lived double lives like my father. Did they throw pans across the room when their wives burned supper? Did they backhand their sons without warning? Did they scream and yell about imaginary wrongs in the middle of the night? Were their children scared of them?"

"I can't imagine, Walter. My father wasn't anything like that."

"You were lucky, Elsie. Most nights Pa went to the tavern after work. Ma and I didn't know whether to wish him home early or late. Too early and he'd be around all night, too late and he came home violent. Either way we were stuck with him. You've got to weather dangerous storms in order to become strong—I learned that from Ma. He was the first dangerous storm I encountered—but he definitely wasn't the last." Walter sent me a knowing look.

"We've seen a few of those storms together now, haven't we?" I dabbed a clean towel on the wound.

"We sure have." Walter gritted his teeth and took the towel from me.

"Do you ever think the world will slow down long enough for us to enjoy each other?"

As Helen's grandfather clock chimed the half hour, Walter rose. "I hope so."

Once the wound had completely dried, I wrapped clean bandages around his arm and helped him put his shirt back on.

"I know where Helen keeps her whiskey," Walter said. "You want to light a fire?"

I wasn't going to sleep any time soon, so I said, "Why not?"

While Walter started a fire in Helen's sitting room, I poured two whiskeys and watched the burgeoning fire dance in our two glasses. I wondered if Helen heard us, but no sound came from upstairs.

"How well do you know these people?"

Walter's back was to me, but he turned and said, "Well enough." I handed him a glass and he sat down on the sofa with me, just an arm's length away.

"Homer Brownfield's the one who introduced me to Kaufmans. Homer wanted to bring their whiskey south from Jackson County into Clinton County, and he needed a driver to do it. That's where I came in. Eventually, word spread that the Brownfield store sold the best whiskey around, and the local speaks began to buy in, too. Now we have distribution in Jackson and Clinton counties and we're starting to deliver into Scott. Driving's good work for me. I've never made more money in my life."

"Aren't you afraid you'll get caught?"

"Nah. I know the back roads better'n anyone. If someone is on my tail, I have more than a dozen stash sites scattered across the tri-county area."

"Is the money really that important?"

When Pa died, he didn't leave us in a good position. A lot of the money I made went to the bank to pay his debts. It left us in a hard place. Somehow the Brownfields knew about the trouble we were having. I don't know if it was Ma. I don't think so, but they found out that our family was struggling. It sure didn't come from me. It got to where Ma owed the Brownfields quite a bit of money. Homer and Rosela let me take home what we needed and just kept a running tab of expenses. Rosela always said, "You'll pay us back when you can." My pride burned hot. I had moved back home to take care of the family, but the sins of my father crippled my efforts. We were drowning." Walter drained his glass. "I can't believe they're gone. Just like that. They weren't bad people."

"You can't kick yourself about the choices you made, Walter. It's not your fault the Brownfields died."

"Some of the blame is mine, Elsie. Nothing you can say will ever change that." Walter poured another whiskey for himself and we talked into the deep of the night.

Tino Cerone

I went underground after the war. That is to say, I stayed in my apartment with the curtains drawn. I shut out the sounds of the city with cotton in my ears and gin in my glass. Noises drove me crazy. Cars backfiring, people yelling, dropped plates breaking, barking dogs, windows slamming, doors creaking, feet running, horses whinnying, pigeons flapping, harbor ships, trolleys, clocks, flags flapping in the wind—they were all the sounds of Mauser fire, mortar, tanks advancing, German giants sailing overhead, U-boat torpedoes, men moaning, limbs getting blown to bits— millions of lives snuffed out. When I finally came out of the apartment and tried life again, I was twenty pounds lighter and whiter than any sheet.

Colosimo was practically a king by then. His racketeering and prostitution rings had grown in my time away, and he even owned a restaurant on South Wabash that pulled in all sorts of famous people. I thought maybe he'd remember me and give me a break. After all, I was a war hero. Well, maybe not a hero, but I had survived.

I stood outside Colosimo's Cafe and straightened my jacket, worked out what I was going to say to him before walking in. I picked up a penny wedged between the cracks in the walk and stashed it in my pocket.

While I stood just outside the front door, several shots were fired inside the building. Any other guy might've run, but I couldn't make myself do anything other than plaster my back up against the wall. More than anything, I wanted to be back at my place, under the covers, with a little cotton and a lot of gin. A screeching sound rang in my ears, like the sound of a freight train hitting the brakes inside a mountain tunnel.

A guy burst through the swinging doors in such a hurry he didn't notice me there.

I stood alone for some time until I realized the sirens were heading my way.

When I got home, I fished the penny out of my pocket, only it wasn't a penny at all, just a token. It said: "Colosimo's Inc. 2126 So Wabash Ave. Good Luck."

At first, everyone thought Colosimo's ex-wife, Victoria Moresco, had him done in. She ran many of his brothels herself and rubbed elbows with some bad sorts. When he divorced her and married Dale Winter, a cabaret singer who worked at his place, Victoria turned into a devil. No evidence ever came out against her though.

To tell the truth, I couldn't even name the guy who shot him. That's the hell of it. It might have been Al Capone. Might have been Frankie Yale from New York. Whoever pulled the trigger, I know who was behind it. Johnny Torrio, Colosimo's underboss, had two reasons to strong arm the business away from him.

First thing was they disagreed about the benefits of Prohibition. Though Colosimo made a pretty penny selling high quality liquor at his restaurant, he fought against expansion. No one knew how serious the law was going to be about illegal distribution. Colosimo was content with what he had and didn't want undue attention, but Torrio knew cashing in on Prohibition was a sure thing—the biggest criminal opportunity in the history of the gang, and he thought Colosimo was a fool not to take the risk.

If Colosimo had done nothing else, he might have survived the disagreement, but Victoria Moresco was Johnny Torrio's aunt, and when he left her, he shamed the family. Torrio no longer had a reason not to step on him. A month after Colosimo married Dale Winter I picked up that token. A month after he married Dale Winter he was dead; a month after he married Dale Winter my plan was over before it began.

Elsie Edens
Wednesday, November 8, 1922

Every moment of light and dark is a miracle.
—Walt Whitman

Though I didn't get to bed until the early morning hours, the rising sun wouldn't allow sleep past sunup; it shone on my torso and called for me to wake. The break of day had scattered the legions of clouds and chased them to the east.

Helen was making coffee on the stove when I came down into the kitchen.

I thanked her for the comfortable bed.

"I'll make you some breakfast, but would you mind going down into the cellar for a new jar of honey?" Helen pointed toward an old wooden door adjacent to the kitchen. "There's a window to the east, should let in enough light for you to see down there."

I took the stairs slowly. Cellars always made my skin crawl a little. Though I was a grown woman, I always moved much faster walking up cellar stairs than I did going down them. My active imagination had me thinking up all sorts of things both human and non.

Any subconscious reservations I had were dispelled by the window's light dancing on hundreds of canning jars. It was a place of sustainable wonder; there were jars of green beans and carrots, potatoes and corn, tomatoes, peaches, apples and jams, and an assortment of other odds and ends I don't recall. What I won't ever forget, though, were the jars of golden honey—stacked twenty long and four deep, slightly dusty from sleep, but filled with sweet promise nonetheless.

I wondered at the amount of honey stashed there. Surely the dozen hives on the lawn couldn't produce that much.

"Where did you get all that honey?" I asked Helen as I emerged from the cellar.

"You saw the hives in the yard, no doubt, but I've more across the river. A dozen more. A healthy hive will produce 200 pounds of honey in a year."

"Surely it will spoil before you use it all?"

"Honey never spoils. They've found edible honey inside the pyramids of Egypt."

"Really?" I thought she might have been pulling my leg, but realized her tone was serious. "How can it last so long?"

"Some say bees are magical. I know my parents thought so. In reality, honey is highly acidic and when stored properly, lacks water. Bacteria can't grow in an environment like that."

"It's fascinating."

As Helen sliced a loaf of fresh bed, I popped the cap on the honey jar and set it on the table.

"The bees I tend immigrated with me, in a way. They are the descendants of those my own great-grandmother kept in England decades ago. Honeybees aren't native to this land."

"I didn't know that."

"People have been bringing them here for so long most people don't, but it's true."

When we finished our breakfast, I tried the phone in Helen's sitting room, but the lines were still down. "Any chance I'll get home today?"

Helen wiped down the table in the kitchen. "Not one. The roads'll need to be passable before they can fix those lines. The sun will help dry things out today, but there's not much wind. You're stuck."

I thanked her again for her hospitality and asked if there was anything I could do to help.

Helen pointed at a bowl of vegetable scraps on the counter and asked if I would feed the chickens. "They're in a pen out back. Go ahead and let them out in the yard. They'll want to forage on this nice day."

She kept seven portly laying hens with striking black-and-white plumage. The fat girls were the same breed my sister, Minnie, kept on her farm when I was young. After I tossed the scraps on the lawn just outside the pen door, the hens strained at the gate. I swung it open and they ran as fast as their bodies would allow, then competed for every scrap.

The county had woken from its rainy sleep, and most of the last leaves that clung to life in the deciduous timber surrounding the two houses had fallen. The day dawned abnormally warm, like late spring. Sparrows flitted about, pecking at the insects that crawled in the damp.

Milkweed pods on the edge of Helen's lawn gave their contents away; seeds embedded in white fluff burst from the insides and hung poised on the verge of goodbye, waiting for a strong wind or a bird to take them to a new home.

While I walked the yard, the radiance of the sun broke through the tree cover and shone on Helen's hives. I had never known someone who kept bees before. The dozen bee boxes were a variety of sizes atop simple four-legged platforms. Some were a foot-and-a-half in height, most were double that. Just above the hive stand, there was a tiny entrance covered by wire mesh with holes only large enough for bees to crawl through.

I didn't expect to see any activity, but a single bee emerged and rose into the air. She flew out a dozen or so feet and back to the hive again. Landing, she crawled to the entrance and began fanning her wings as quickly as if she were flying, though she didn't move from the spot. Several other bees performed the same maneuver. They flew a short distance away, then returned to mimic her.

As I crouched next to a hive on the end, Helen approached.

"I'm surprised they're still flying this late in the fall," I said.

"It's warm enough they're taking the opportunity to get rid of waste. She crouched down next to me. You see these ladies here?" She pointed at those fanning their wings.

"Why are they doing that?"

"As long as they have food, bees can tolerate even the harshest of winters. It's moisture that kills them. The bees are fanning in order to dehumidify the air in the hive."

"What's the wire mesh for?"

Helen stood and approached the next hive, brushing a few dead bees from the platform. "Mice will take up residence in a hive as soon as the weather turns. They'll eat the honey, the wax, and even the bees themselves to stay alive. If mice get in, the hive will die."

"Can't the bees just sting them?"

"They'll surround and kill a mouse in the summer months. They're strong and active then, but in the winter, they're clustered for warmth. Their only movement is to shiver around the queen to keep her alive."

"What about now? In November?"

"I suppose that depends on the day. If it's a warm day, they can take care of themselves. See this one here?" Helen pointed at a bee standing at attention just inside the entrance. "That's a guard. It's her job to watch out for thieves like mice and wasps. If one comes near, she'll warn the others and they'll swarm."

Later that morning, the siblings gathered for a private meeting in Helen's kitchen to discuss how they were going to proceed.

Walter and I needed to find something to do for a while, and he led me through the timber behind Helen's house.

The chance to pass the morning with a leisurely walk, one not tied to the tailing of a suspect or the tracking down of information, was something I hadn't done in a long while.

We were headed down a steep footpath in the opposite direction of the town, toward the Maquoketa River that ran a half-mile or so from the town center. Fallen leaves lined our path, allowing us to walk above the mud. The only color was afforded by the occasional evergreen. Their uppermost needles slow-danced in the slight breeze. Squirrels darted about, displacing damp leaves in search of acorn and hickory nuts.

The descending path wound its way into the woods for a few hundred yards until we emerged from it alongside a flat field of harvested corn. The shorn stalks still held fast to the earth by prop roots that grasped like fingers. On the other side of the field, just before the timber began again, two does raised their heads to look at us and bounded into the trees. Their white tails were visible for a moment then disappeared entirely.

"Walter, what do you think the Kaufmans are going to do?"

We wove around a few scrubby red cedar trees growing in the grasses along the field. Their evergreen branches were thick and hardy.

"I don't know for sure. Stanley asked me a lot of questions after the meeting at Helen's yesterday, but he didn't let on what he was thinking."

"What did he ask you?"

"He asked me to repeat everything. He wanted to know exactly what the guy said to me. What he looked like. What kind of car he drove. About his gun, his manner. Whether or not I saw anyone else with him."

"Is that all?"

"He asked me some questions about you."

"What kind of questions?"

We reached the end of the field, near the animal path the deer had taken. I heard the rush of water, but I couldn't see the river yet.

"He wanted to know more about our past together. How I know you. What kind of person you are."

"And what did you tell him?" I stopped. Suddenly, I was worried that Walter might have let something slip. If he was worried that the Kaufmans wouldn't trust me, would he be willing to share something of what happened so long ago in order to gain their trust?

"I know what you're thinking, Elsie." Walter stopped. "I wouldn't tell anyone about that, ever."

I believed him and felt foolish for suspecting but needed to explain myself. "You mentioned my ability to keep secrets to them yesterday. It just made me nervous."

"That was a reference to your job, not our past."

I hung my head, ashamed I had let my guilt take charge once again.

Walter reached out and raised my chin, so our eyes met. "You've nothing to feel guilty about. I don't either. No one does except the guy who killed Minnie, and he's dead."

The thought of him seared and burned in my mind, bringing back the image of his leering face when he found

Walter and me hiding under the bed. My right hand flew up to my neck in an attempt to protect it from the memory of him strangling me. To this day, I can't abide anyone touching my neck. I react immediately and violently, lashing out at the offender without realizing what I'm doing. I can't help it.

Walter brought me toward him and we gave each other a half hug, avoiding his wounded arm. As we did so, I remembered that my sister, Minnie, and I weren't the only ones hurt by her murderer. I leaned back and touched the spot above Walter's right eye that had once been so badly bruised.

Some distance away we saw three men working their way through the trees. They plodded down a different path on the way back to Hurstville.

Walter smiled down at me, and I felt he was older than I was somehow, though I was four years his senior. "I have something to show you, Elsie."

"What is it?"

"I saw you looking at Helen's bees earlier."

"You were watching me?"

Walter looked at the men, their backs disappearing into the trees. "Do you want to see the rest of the hives?"

I couldn't deny it. The bees were fascinating.

We walked toward the Maquoketa River, a wild and winding thing running southeasterly and known for its shallow runs and occasionally unpredictable depths. With the recent rains it was flowing quickly, deep and dark with earth and tree limbs—a good 70 feet wide or more.

When we broke from the trees and out onto the riverbank, Walter turned to a mound and began tossing branches aside. Before long, a canoe was unearthed from its hiding place. Walter helped me in and shoved it out into the current a little before hopping in himself. I grabbed an oar.

"You don't mind?"

"You certainly won't be much help in a sling," I said.

"Do you know how to steer a canoe?"

"I'm perfectly capable, Mr. Winkle," I said, and settled into the back of the canoe. My brother John had a pond behind his place and a favorite summer activity of mine was taking the thing out myself, dropping an oar in the middle of the pond, and whiling the day away with a book. *Last of the Mohicans, Treasure Island, 20,000 Leagues Under the Sea.* To take time out with a good book is a vacation unto itself, but to do so in that place was pure heaven. The action of those tales played itself out on the glassy surface of that pond and mesmerized me better than the picture shows in movie houses.

Walter explained, "There used to be a bridge here some years ago, but they dismantled it."

"What in the world for?" I asked.

"Bernard's stills are across the river, too."

The bridge, Walter explained, had been taken down in order to prevent the authorities from finding the stills. Access from the other side of the river was difficult, if not impossible, due to the heavy undergrowth beneath the trees—thick, thorny, and riddled with poison ivy, no place anyone wanted to trek through. Bernard wanted it that way. The only way to the stills was from the river side, and although it was easy enough for someone who was looking to travel downstream and dock a small boat on shore, there were few people on the river who weren't already employed by the Kaufmans in some way. The bridge from Hurstville was the only realistic way anyone would find the stills, so Bernard and Stanley had taken it down the day after the stills were set up across the river. Bernard and his men made their way back and forth in canoes. A pontoon was used when liquor was ready for transport.

As our canoe drifted, mink and muskrat slid into secret havens around us. In the turbid waters below, catfish and bullhead swayed in the current. The river carried us downstream, but I was able to steer the canoe to the opposite side without difficulty.

Like a sleek river otter, the craft ran up the bank. Walter got out and pulled the canoe in so the current couldn't sweep it away before I was able to get out. The river mud oozed underneath my boots and threatened to suck them in before I stepped onto a dense patch of water grass that held me aloft. Walter hauled the craft beyond the flood line where another canoe rested underneath a camouflage of bare brambles and branches. Walter took some time to cover the boat while I was distracted by a bald eagle following the river just below the treetops.

Thanks to a crude stone stairway, we emerged atop a steep bank into the wilds of what Walter called Little Oklahoma. He couldn't tell me why the locals called it that, but it was a term of endearment for a place that brought life back into a dwindling community and kept the wolf away from the door. Dense undergrowth and heavy timber compelled us to stay on the path as a soft wind whispered from within the bare trees, and a myriad of invisible birds called out like a spell from *Grimm's Fairytales*.

After a few minutes' walk, we emerged into a clearing about half the size of a town block. Bee boxes stood as sentinels for the area, spaced out in fifty-foot intervals on three sides. Their fronts faced out into the timber, like a warning for passersby. The warmth of the day brought bees from the hives, just a few here and there on a short path from the box and back. More of the mums were planted between each hive, a low barrier to the wild parts of the area and far enough away from the surrounding trees to gather just enough light. They were spindly, though, not like the lush blooms that lined the driveway to Helen's house.

Limestone boulders as tall as Walter and I covered the space to the east above which towered a rocky cliff face a hundred or so feet above our heads. Red cedar and northern pin oak strove for a home in the cracks and crevices. All other sides of the expanse were hugged by trees and brush. At one time the area had been blasted for lime, but when production slowed, so did the need to pull stone from across the river. There were more convenient quarries elsewhere, and the hidden area we walked along was needed as a secret place for distillation. Due to the heavy traffic in its past, the inner portion of the clearing was mostly devoid of plant life, its surface blanketed by limestone gravel and boot tracks.

There were two unpainted barns in the area, each large enough in which to park four or five autos with plenty of elbow room besides. The first was used for the distillation of whiskey, the second for aging.

On the far side of the clearing was Bernard's modest cabin and a shed near it, about half as large as the barns. Both cabin and shed were of a darker wooden hue than the rest of the buildings on the site, so had the look of age like those in Hurstville proper.

Cordwood was stacked between the two larger sheds along with a smaller pile near the cabin.

Also near the barns was a windmill that reached higher than the trees. Alongside it, a wooden water tower sat as well, with a pipe running into one of the buildings. An exterior spigot protruded just above a wide stone sink.

A boy lay propped against the metal posts of the windmill, dark hat covering his eyes and a large yellow cat sound asleep on his lap. Walter reached down and picked up a rock. He gave it a gentle underhand toss and it landed right on the brim of the boy's hat. Neither boy nor cat woke, so Walter repeated the maneuver until there were several rocks nestled on the hat, a few wayward pebbles rolling off near the cat's head or tail. Walter and I laughed so hard we nearly bowled ourselves over in the yellow dust.

One of us shifted our feet in the gravel, which woke the boy and caused the cat to scamper off underneath Bernard's front porch.

"Jesus, Walter!" The boy scrambled to his feet, slipping twice on the loose ground before he was able to stand up straight. His hat fell off, dispersing the rocks and revealing a mop of brown hair and grey eyes. There was no doubt he was the son of Alice, the shopkeeper I'd met the day before. Their facial features were uncannily similar. "What are you doing here?"

"We were hoping you could help us, Roy."

"Me?"

"Yeah, you." Walter was playing him. Roy wasn't more than thirteen and served as lookout for the distillery during the day. With noon approaching, most of the men who worked for Bernard on this side of the river were home for lunch.

"I thought you might be able to give my friend, Elsie, a tour of the facilities."

Roy grabbed his hat and brushed the yellow dust from its brim and underside. Placing it on his head, he affected authority. "I'm not so sure Mr. Kaufman would approve."

"Bernard isn't here though, is he? Who's inside right now?"

"My brother."

Walter laughed. "Raymond won't mind. I know that for a fact."

Walter was right. When Roy let us in the door, Raymond was checking the temperature gauge on one of the eight copper stills that lined the walls of the building. He turned and brightened at Walter's presence. Walter and Raymond shook hands and gave each other hard pats on the back.

"You take care of that problem?" Raymond asked Walter, winking.

"Taken care of."

I'd no idea what Raymond was asking about and looked at Walter for some sign, but he gave none.

"And who's this?"

"This is Elsie Edens."

I held out my hand.

Raymond hesitated, unsure of what to do with it, but I grasped his and shook it. He smiled and looked to Walter. Red splotches of color bloomed over his neck and crawled into his cheeks. "R . . . Raymond Henderson," he said.

"I met your mother," I said. "I assume Alice is your mother?"

"How did you guess?" Raymond gave me a wry smile.

He looked much like his mother and brother. He had the same brown hair and grey eyes, but his face was scruffy with stubble and he was years older, probably Walter's age. "You'll be wanting a tour, then?"

"That's right," Walter said.

"Be happy to, but we'd better hurry it up. The guys'll be back soon enough." He looked to Roy. "Keep a lookout for them."

Roy opened his mouth to protest, but Raymond held up his hand. "If you want to keep your job, you'll go back to it."

Back in his element, Raymond shed all awkwardness. He explained that the chief distiller was Bernard, but that Raymond and a crew of other men participated in one or more parts of the production of whiskey, from picking corn to bottling. Raymond proceeded to talk me through the process, one built from the ground up by townspeople who had become experts in every part of it.

"The recipe begins with a mash of sugar, water, yeast, and ground corn. Corn's grown right here by Hurstville's farmers. We cook the mash and pour it into barrels for fermentation, keeping it right inside the shed here where the temperature is warm due to the heat coming off the stills. The warmer it is, the sooner it's ready." Raymond popped the lid off one of the fermenting barrels. Inside was a dark yellow frothy stuff, bubbling much like mother's stovetop porridge, but smelling like her sourdough bread. "During fermentation, the yeast breaks the starches down into sugars. One result of that chemical reaction is alcohol." Raymond beamed at me and winked.

Walter gave him a playful punch to the arm.

Raymond secured the lid. "Days later, the juice from the mixture is strained and placed in the copper stills here." Raymond gestured to one of the 100-gallon stills, each of which stood taller than any of us and gleamed red-gold. "These are made by the men who work at the hardware store in town. They also inspect the stills for leaks and repair them when necessary."

He continued. "Next, the alcohol is separated from the mash. This is called distillation. Water boils at 212 degrees, but alcohol boils at 172. If the temperature is maintained, only the alcohol steam is boiled off. The steam from the mash is diverted through this copper cap arm." Raymond pointed to a fat pipe that protruded from the top of the still and ran a right angle down into a smaller copper keg.

"This little guy is called the thump keg. The liquid in the keg takes the heated steam and filters out any impurities that may have gotten through. Hear that?" Raymond cupped his hand at his ear. A soft plunk or thump came from the bottom of the keg. "That sound is made when the steam is forced under the warm liquid in there. The alcohol steam is then re-evaporated and pure."

Another copper pipe ran from the top of the thump keg and into a barrel. Inside the barrel the coil wound down like a snake through circulating cool water. "The steam is forced through this copper coil. We call it the worm. The cooling process condenses the mixture from a gas into a liquid." Raymond bent over and pointed at a clear liquid dripping from a short copper tube and into another barrel.

"Why is it clear?" I asked. The liquid I saw in the jars at the Brownfield store and again at Mave's was a dark gold.

"There are a couple more steps to our recipe—honey and time. Those bee boxes aren't just for show," Raymond explained. "Honey is the magic ingredient. When distillation is complete, we make honey syrup. Just a little honey and water added to the whiskey and you've got a match made in heaven. This charred oak barrel," Raymond patted the side of the receptacle like the back of a loved child, "will age the mixture for up to a year."

Walter explained, "The cooper shop in Hurstville has been making oak barrels for decades. That's what they transport the lime in. It's the perfect cover, really."

"Where is it aged?" I asked.

"In the other barn here. The temperature difference coaxes the young moonshine into mature whiskey. All whiskey starts out as moonshine. It just needs a little love and some experience to come out playing nice."

"I know what you mean," I said. "I've tasted it. It's smooth and sweet."

"Once it's matured, we keep the stuff in cold storage. There's a cave on site here that doesn't fluctuate in temperature no matter what time of year it is."

The shed door swung open and a wide-eyed Roy slid in. "They're coming! You'd better go!"

Walter grasped my hand.

"Hide behind the honey shed until they've come inside," Raymond said.

Walter nodded. As we ran out, I turned my head and thanked him. He returned my thanks with another wink.

Walter took me to the opposite side of the clearing, behind the shed that stood nearest Bernard's cabin. From around the corner of the shed we watched five men emerge from the timber, along a different path than we had taken earlier, but not so far from it. It appeared as if the men were heading straight for the building we had just come from. One of them broke from the group, however, fiddling with his belt and heading in our general direction.

Walter led me to the side closest to the cabin where he quietly unlatched the wooden door and followed me into the darkened shed. There were many empty glass jars lining the counter and a wood stove with pots on top. We crouched there, so as not to be seen through the window on the opposite side. The man passed in front of the window, and shortly after, we heard him urinating.

He had finished and was on his way to join the others when Walter stood abruptly and clambered back toward the door. "Holy!"

"What is it?" I asked. I stood as well, not knowing what he had seen.

"Look at that!" Walter pointed at a hairy wolf spider, approximately two inches round, that had emerged from behind crates and barrels stacked underneath a wooden counter. It was frozen in place just a foot away from Walter's shoe as we hid.

Wolf spiders aren't at all poisonous, but I'd known someone who'd been bitten by one. My brother, Christ, had attempted to make one his pet when we were kids. He kept it in a cigar box for two days, cracking the lid every now and again. The poor thing huddled in the corner until the third day as Christ gawked at it while sitting on the front stoop. Hungry and thirsty, it bit Christ's pointer finger when he waggled it inside the box. Startled, Christ tossed the box to the ground and the wolf spider high-tailed it underneath the porch.

The bite, Christ said, felt something like a bee sting, sudden and painful. He had no adverse reaction to it and forgot about the whole thing the next morning.

Occasionally, we found one in the cellar, usually in the fall. I'd taken a liking to the things, I suppose, hearing once that it was bad luck to kill a spider. Fedelma may have been the one to tell me that. I don't remember anymore.

Walter looked around for a lengthy weapon with which to crush it. I grabbed a glass canning jar from the counter and lowered it over the top of the spider.

"Now what?" Walter asked.

"Now I let it outside," I said. I took my notebook and slid its hardback cover underneath the jar. The spider lifted its legs and scrambled on top of it. Holding the notebook securely underneath the jar, I carried the temporary sanctuary to the door. "Open it a crack."

"Why don't you just smash the thing?"

"They're not pests, Walter. Not any more than you and I."

"I'm going to have to disagree with you on that one."

I turned the jar right side up, sliding the spider down to the bottom of the jar. Its long legs nearly touched the sides. "See, it's harmless," I told him, holding it up so Walter could see.

"Get that thing away from me!" Walter backed up into the counter, sending several empty jars rattling.

Laughing, I held the jar on its side near the door and tipped it gently. We watched as the spider walked right back out into the world.

"I hope I never see anything like that ever again."

"That's wishful thinking, Walter. Wolf spiders are pretty common in Iowa."

"I don't want to hear it. I'd rather forget they exist."

You'd think, after the people of the United States came together and fought in the war to end all wars, they would have found a common thread to tie them all together. Instead of The Great War uniting some people, however, it divided them even further, resulting in ugly scraps of fabric—stained, fraying, and threadbare.

The Ku Klux Klan was one of the ugliest scraps, infested with fleas that fed on the fears of others. They weren't just afraid of colored people, but also Catholics, Jews, and immigrants. The irony of the last, given their own ancestry, apparently never occurred to them.

In 1915, a film called *The Birth of a Nation* encouraged a resurgence of Klan membership. The three-hour saga showed blacks as aggressive and stupid and white men as heroic saviors of demure white ladies. I've been told the producer wasn't racist himself, but his storytelling was so effective that the dramatic scenes in the fictional tale stirred up old fears and had millions of men signing up for Klan membership.

The film played in Des Moines in 1916, intensifying racist feeling in Iowa. The National Association for the Advancement of Colored People had organized in Des Moines in 1915, so their protest of the film was one of the group's first actions in the state. They were concerned, and rightly so, that the movie would embolden supremacists into action.

A couple of years after the Brownfield murders, annual klonklaves took place right in Jackson County, at the fairgrounds just three miles away from Hurstville. Thousands of men, women, and children attended. The third annual event brought in an estimated eight thousand. Bands played, male quartets sang, and food was served before an evening naturalization ritual that began with the burning of three towering crosses. New members were sworn in while children played in the grasses beyond Gibson field.

With more than four million members nationwide, the Klan influenced local and national elections. Lesser known, perhaps, was the KKK's involvement in the Eighteenth Amendment. They supported what they called "clean living" and spoke against drinking and other behavior they deemed scandalous. Once the new law was in place, Klan members accompanied authorities on still raids and actively sought out nightclubs and speakeasies in certain areas of Iowa.

Thankfully, there were organizations in addition to the NAACP that still had sense and spoke out against the Klan. The American Legion, the Masons, and Farm Bureau opposed the KKK, though the Legion was the most vocal. In Des Moines, the Legion encouraged the Yenter Anti-Mask Bill, making it a misdemeanor to wear a mask and prowl around with the intention of harassing others.

In 1922, the local Klan was more than a nuisance. A cancer, really—easier to ignore than confront and just as deadly.

Walter and I returned from our tour of the distillery and walked straight into Hurstville for lunch at the café there. Alice greeted us and poured large glasses of iced tea while we waited for our sandwiches. Two men sat at the counter a few seats down from us. They had finished their lunches and one of them chewed loudly on a piece of hard candy from the bowl Alice had set on the counter. It was filled with the assorted candies mother also served at the hotel, blue-and-white striped, green pinwheels, red-and-white folded ribbons, and more.

They talked loudly, and it was impossible not to eavesdrop. It became clear they were from Iowa, though not from Hurstville proper. Alice showed Walter and me a quick smile and was friendly enough, though she seemed to be agitated by the presence of the two men. She slopped coffee on the counter and had difficulty making change for them.

After Alice walked into the back room, Marcus entered and immediately took off his hat. He wiped his feet on the rug, perhaps more so than necessary, and approached Walter and me.

The older of the two men stared at Marcus and popped an orange candy into his mouth. "What are you doing in here?"

Marcus rubbed the brim of his hat and ignored the question, addressing Walter and me. "The meeting's over. Helen said you're welcome to come back to the house when you're ready."

The man stood up, his fork clattering to the floor. "This is no place for a nigger. We're eating here."

Marcus was careful not to look at him, but Walter rose from his seat, his one hand supporting his sling as he did so. "That's not how things are done here."

"It should be," the younger man said, though he remained seated.

"In this place," Walter said, "my friend here is welcome. You, on the other hand . . ."

Alice came from the back room with our plates, though she didn't set them on the counter.

"Look, I don't want any trouble." Marcus gestured to Alice. "Mrs. Henderson doesn't deserve such in her place. I've done what I came here for, so I'll be leaving."

"Wait a minute," the older man said. "You look familiar. Doesn't this nigger look familiar, Andy?"

"Now that you mention it, he does look familiar."

"Seems you look just like the man wanted for a robbery at the Savannah Savings Building and Loan across the river."

"He sure does, Cain. He looks just like the guy on the poster we saw."

"I've never stepped foot in Savannah, don't even know where that is," Marcus said.

"We could use that $1,000 reward." Andy rose, his chair teetering slightly from the abrupt move.

"Now just wait a minute," I broke in. I'd heard enough. It was clear the two just wanted to start trouble. The man wanted for the Savannah robbery was a colored man, but Marcus' features did not match those in the posters plastered up and down both sides of the river. "I've seen those posters, and he doesn't look a thing like him."

"You calling us liars, Miss?" Cain took a step forward.

Walter advanced toward the man, stopping just a few feet from physical confrontation. Now that he was in front of me, I noticed that Walter's good hand rested on a gun he had tucked into the back of his pants. "I think you'll want to move on now, before something happens that you'll regret."

Cain's eyes lowered. "You tell Stanley if he doesn't get this place in shape, the Klan won't look the other way anymore. You tell him that."

While the men walked out, Andy sang, "On a hill far away burns a bright fiery cross, the emblem of those that are free—" The door slammed behind him.

Alice let out a long breath. "I'm very sorry about that. Those two have been stuck here since yesterday, too."

"Where are they from?" I asked.

"Sabula, east of here," Alice said.

I knew Sabula. It was on the Iowa side of the Mississippi, across the river from Savannah, Illinois. "What did he mean about the Klan not looking the other way anymore?"

Marcus explained, "Stanley pays the Klan to keep quiet about the operation here. He knows some of the higher-ups. He doesn't agree with their views, but a while back they caught wind of the whiskey business and threatened to turn us all in."

Tino Cerone

After Colosimo's death, I thought my prospects with the gang were over. I found work at Sabella's Meat Market, hauling cattle and hog carcasses off trucks, hacking them down into rump, rib, flank. Grinding the meat, making sausages, covering myself in blood.

Blocks of ice from Lake Michigan were hauled in from storage sheds to keep the meat fresh. The thickness of the ice shut out the sounds of the street and the freezing air quieted the spells that came over me. I got used to being alone in that cold room.

I got used to the slippery floors, the scent of blood in the air.

I got used to the knives. Sharp and glistening.

Like hibernation.

Carmine Sabella and his nephew ran the front of the shop and waited on customers. I knew Sabella was in with Torrio and the gang. Everyone knew that, but his legitimate business ran so smoothly, I had no idea how well he was connected until I saved Johnny Torrio's life.

That day started like this.

Sabella poked his head in back as I put my apron on for the day's bloody work. His baggy eyes made him look tired all the time. Tall fella. Said his nephew wouldn't be in; the wife was birthing a child. He needed me to package meat out front for customers.

I was hanging hunks of meat up in the store window when Johnny Torrio walked by.

He was easy to spot. Looked like a banker. The Fox, people called him. Smart and sneaky.

Torrio insisted all his men dress and act like the businessmen they were. Sharp dress. Clean speech. Legitimate front. Fly as far below the radar as possible. Don't act like a thug and you won't be treated like one, Torrio said.

He had a couple of guys with him, and I thought he was just going to keep on moving down the street, only he stepped in the store. Sabella made a big to-do over it. They hugged, clapped each other on the back. "It's time for us to talk about the next step," Torrio said to him.

Sabella offered to take him for coffee next door.

"Nah, nah," Torrio said. "You'll come over to the house tonight. We'll talk."

Lucky for Torrio his two men were between him and the door.

A car pulled up out front; a single guy got out, and in plain sight let loose with a six shooter that killed the two men Torrio was with and sent Torrio and Sabella sprawling. The glass from the front window shattered all over the floor. I don't remember taking cover, but somehow I ended up on my back behind the counter, hands up over my ears, glass slicing through my shirt.

Torrio yelled. "You tell that rat bastard—"

He didn't finish whatever it was he wanted to say. The gunman's feet crunched over broken glass and he tried to pop off a shot, but there was only a click. Then another.

I realized what I had there was a chance. I felt for the cleaver I'd left on the counter and pulled myself up. Torrio and Sabella were scrambling over the glass as the gunman reloaded. He didn't even know I was there until I rose up behind him and buried the cleaver right between his shoulder blades.

Life moves on like that until you don't even know yourself any more.

Elsie Edens
Thursday, November 9, 1922

When we try to pick out anything by itself, we find it hitched to everything else in the Universe.
—John Muir

Do you ever get so scared in your dreams you wake yourself up? In his *Interpretation of Dreams,* Sigmund Freud said a dream is a wish fulfilled. That's a bunch of hooey if you ask me. Apparently, the man never had a nightmare in his life. On the other hand, I do think he was onto something when he wrote about the value of dreams. I don't think they are meaningless mind matter, but a representation of something important. Interpret me this, Freud:

In this dream, a man fastened a wooden swing from the largest branch of my sister's maple tree. I couldn't see his face at first, his wide-brimmed hat covered it. Minnie stood with hands on hips while a much younger me tried it out. I shoved my dress under my knees, lest the man should catch a glimpse of my underthings. It was hard to pump any momentum while trying to maintain decorum. Minnie laughed at my concern and ran forward to give me a push. The man stepped in to help, he and Minnie taking turns, and it wasn't until then I knew he was her killer. In the dream, Minnie was dressed in black and he in white, but I know in reality their souls were the other way around. Each time the swing reached its highest point I heard a crack, crack, crack as the chain rubbed against the bark of the tree. It became so loud it frightened me, and I screamed at them to stop. They only laughed together, however, and shoved me even higher. I knew something bad was going to happen. I was going to hit my head on the large branches above or fly out of the seat and break bones. Then Mother was up in the tree and she tried to grasp my hand, pull me up to her safe perch, but I couldn't grab hold, barely brushing her fingertips. Their figures became smaller and smaller, and I just kept rising until I couldn't see anyone anymore. I don't know what held me in place, for it couldn't have been the tree. Perhaps it was the stars. Maybe it was nothing at all.

When I woke from it, I heard the crack again. The same sound in my dream rose through the windows in my room. It was a gunshot, and it startled my addled brain into action. I stumbled to the window.

Out on the lawn, Helen stood with her hands raised. She'd a tight wool cap on her head and a small black gun in her hand. I watched her load a round of bullets and send seven shots into a dirt bank covered with food cans, sand-filled flour sacks, and an old metal butter churn.

I dressed in my own dry clothes and snatched a biscuit and cup of strong coffee from the kitchen, then walked out to the front porch. The steam from my cup rose and curled around the porch beams.

"You ever shoot one of these?" she called to me while loading it again.

At that point, I had never shot a gun, period. Wits over arms, I thought. Phinny always carried one and kept it in a chest holster at all times, but I'd never seen him use it. I *had* killed a man already. I already told you that. I was afraid that a gun would make it all too easy to do it again.

"This is called a vest pocket pistol," Helen said. "Though it'll fit nicely in a number of ladies' garments." She opened her palm and showed me the thing, so small a large man could have concealed it within his palm. Its grip was textured, crisscrossed with grooves and adorned with a rearing horse. "Colt" was printed on the handle. "Holds seven if you put one in the chamber."

"It's so small."

"It might be that, but if you're within ten to fifteen feet and know where to aim, you'll kill a man."

"What did you decide to do about the gang?" I asked her.

Helen aimed at the low hill covered in makeshift targets already littered with numerous bullet holes. She squeezed the rear safety and sent two bullets into a large tin can. It toppled over and rolled down to the yellowed grass on the far side. "We decided we need your help."

"In what way?" I asked.

"I need you to let me know if the investigation into the deaths of Homer and Rosela leads the sheriff here." Helen sent two more bullets into the debris.

"I won't reveal anything about you to the authorities," I promised. And I meant it. There was no reason to, at least not yet. The Kaufmans weren't suspects.

"I don't think you will," she said, "but can you also keep an ear out for what the authorities know? Hurstville can't afford another blow. It's not just about my brothers and me; it's about everyone who lives here."

Somewhere behind me, through the trees and below the hill, school-age children laughed at one another. A mother's voice scolded, followed by more laughter from the children.

"I can do that," I said, though I agreed to do it more for Walter than for anyone else. "And what will you do if Cerone's people find you?"

"We'll deal with that if it comes," Helen said.

"Even if Walter disappears for a while, it's only a matter of time until they track the whiskey back here."

Another bullet was buried in a sand-filled sack.

"You handle keeping the law out of our backyard. We'll take care of the rest." She motioned for me to join her. "Come give the Colt a little spin."

Although I never answered Helen when she asked me if I'd shot a pocket pistol before, I'm sure she knew quickly I'd never shot any kind of gun at all. She was patient with me, though, and showed me how to grip and aim. I was no Annie Oakley, but managed to at least hit the dirt bank the targets were propped up on.

"A woman in your profession ought to have a gun," she said.

"So I've been told."

"I don't know what your reason is, but from where I stand it's a damn fool one. That knife I've seen you playing with requires you to get much too close to an attacker. Best to fend him off before he gets near you."

I started to offer an explanation, but just then Walter came out to Stanley's front porch and called out.

"Phones are up!" He pulled up his suspender straps, hair still disheveled from sleep.

"I have my reasons," I said.

The long-distance call took some time for the operator to hook up, so by the time I was finally connected to Mama, I'd finished my second cup of coffee.

"Where in heaven's name have you been?" she asked.

I knew she worried about me enough as it was, but I'd dropped off the map since Monday morning.

"I walked over to your office both Tuesday and Wednesday afternoons, but Phinny didn't answer," she said. "I assumed you were both out of town on a case, and you forgot to tell me." Mama sighed heavily into the phone. "I'll never get used to your choice of profession."

It was odd Phinny had not answered. He rarely left the place anymore, even had a young man deliver groceries from the corner store.

I apologized to mother and explained the basic situation having to do with the impassable roads, my marooned auto, and the downed phone lines, though I certainly didn't go into detail beyond that. I tried to wrap up the conversation, explaining to her that I'd likely be on the road within 24 hours. My auto was still in the ditch, but if the phone company was able to fix the lines, the roads were reasonably passable, and I hoped someone could haul it out for me.

"There was a gentleman asking for you," Mama said.

"What man?" Given mother's choice of words, I assumed right away it must be someone looking to ask me to a picture show. There were a couple of local boys who wouldn't take no for an answer. I'd no patience for such things.

"He's stayed for nearly a week. Came last Thursday, I think. Frank Rossi. You may have seen him in the dining room. That's where he saw you."

"Come on, Mama. You know I'm not interested in men right now."

"He's handsome. A salesman. Successful if looks can be any indication of that."

"Like I said, Mama—"

"Had some terrible marks on him, though. Can't imagine how he got those."

"What?"

"I told him my daughter's going to get in over her head one of these days."

"I wish you wouldn't talk to people about me. Especially strangers."

"I didn't see the harm in telling him you worked for Mr. Lawrence. The whole town knows anyway." Mama called out to Doris, the young maid, "Don't forget to take out the rubbish! Anyway, he's gone now. Left unexpectedly on Tuesday and I haven't seen him since, so the point is moot."

I tried to wrap up the conversation, explaining my need to check in with Phinny. Trying to bring a conversation to a close with Mama was nearly impossible, however. A conversation wasn't over until she decided it was.

"Since you won't tell me where you are, I don't know if you've heard the latest on the Brownfield murders."

"I know they caught the man who likely did it."

"They may have reeled him in, but he got away."

"What are you talking about?"

"So you haven't heard, then. A deputy tried to bring him in Monday night, but they never made it to the station. He's probably long gone by now."

Mama prattled on, but a thousand and one questions ran through my mind and they did so behind a veil of red. That idiot, Mandersheid, had somehow let him go. I interrupted her, "Did he hurt anyone?"

"The paper didn't mention anyone was hurt, just that the man got away."

"Is there any more news?"

"Not that I know of. Nothing in this morning's paper, anyway."

"Please don't worry about me, Mama. I'll see you as soon as I can."

"No use telling me that. I know you're involved, though you told me otherwise. I *will* worry until you call again. There's nothing you can do about that."

"I'm sorry, Mama. I've got to go."

I hung up on her and called Phinny immediately.

Phinny picked up sounding tired, reluctant, and angry all at once.

"I've been waiting for you," he said.

"I'm sorry. I have a lot to tell you. A lot has happened."

"I haven't heard from you for days. Also, I have a . . ." Phinny hesitated, "guest."

A new voice came onto the phone just then. A voice scratchy from overuse or too many cigarettes. A voice I recognized. "I'm here with your boss, and you know how I found him?" He didn't pause for an answer. "Your mother's been kind enough to put me up. Sure is a nice little place."

Walter and Helen came in from outside and headed into the kitchen.

Frank Rossi was Henry Barzetti was Tino Cerone. "Cerone. I know who you are."

"Your move, Miss Edens."

A choking sensation came over me and I had trouble speaking. "If you hurt Phinny or my mother, I'll—"

Walter approached, followed by Helen who wrung a towel in her hands.

"I will if the law finds out, so watch what you say," Cerone said. I knew his threat was twofold. I couldn't alert the authorities and also had to be careful what information was shared over the phone. Nosy operators could listen in, as well as any one of the many individuals attached to Helen's community phone line.

I cleared my throat. "What do you want?"

"The kid already knows what I want. I've sent word back to Chicago about what's going on here in Iowa. They expect a shipment now, and I'm going to give it to them. I have no choice, so you have no choice."

"If all you want is a shipment, why did you do it?" Despite admitting to the murders, he was maintaining his story: They just wanted to do business.

"Until we're partners, we're enemies, Miss. He wasn't interested in giving me the information I needed, neither was his wife. I want to meet these people. We have business to discuss."

My brain leaped to the incomprehensible visual of Mama and Phinny in the positions of Rosela and Homer Brownfield. Despite my horror at that idea, I couldn't give Cerone what he wanted by myself. I had to discuss a plan with Walter and the Kaufmans. "I'm not in a position to negotiate this right now," I replied.

"Then you'd better find someone who can and quick."

"I'll have to call you back." It was painful to say so, but there was no other way around it.

"I'll expect your call within the hour. I meet the distillers today. That's not negotiable. No law. Things don't happen my way and we know how to get to the people you love."

Cerone hung up the phone. It didn't occur to me until much later that C. Auguste Dupin hadn't made a sound.

As the Kaufman siblings and Marcus gathered in Helen's kitchen, I paced the floor.

"I'm so sorry, Elsie." Walter reached out to touch my arm, and I recoiled. A buzzing sound began growing in my ears.

"I'll kill him myself," Bernard said.

"That's a little hasty considering the fact that he's not working alone, brother," Stanley said. "We have Elsie's people to think about."

"We have this community to think about," Helen said. "Violence has to be a last resort."

Stanley thought the best thing was to play along with Cerone and give him what he said he wanted, a shipment of honey whiskey to take back to Chicago. "If we don't do as he asked . . ." He didn't finish that thought, but we all knew what that could mean. "Given Elsie's last conversation, I think it's possible they really do want to do business with us. We have to start thinking about the long-term here. With the Brownfields gone, we've lost quite a bit of our revenue."

Helen suggested we meet Cerone on the south side of Maquoketa. "I don't want him anywhere near this place," she said.

"If things get ugly, we'll have a lot more control over the outcome if we're here," Bernard argued.

"Control?" Helen said. "We have a town of people to think about! What happens if he brings more men and they start shooting?"

Marcus agreed with her. "It's probably not a good idea to expose our location, either."

The buzzing grew to such a decibel, I couldn't take it anymore. I shook my head and tapped my fingers on my ears.

"Are you all right?" Walter asked.

Without answering, I walked out onto Helen's porch. The morning was much too cold to be outside without a coat, but I didn't notice the chill. Walter followed me and said some things, but I didn't hear him. I had a sense that I was swimming out to sea, leaving loved ones behind—swimming directly out into the deep blue while mute friends and family members called for me to stop. I don't know how long I stayed out there, swimming.

Walter left me at some point. I know he thought I was angry with him, but something was working itself out in my head.

Moisture glistened on the tops of Helen's bee boxes. It was too chilly for the bees to defend themselves that morning, but once again the day warmed, adding another sigh of Indian summer. As the sun rose, more and more bees would venture out to see what the day had in store.

Bees have many enemies—wasps, mice, rival hives, humans, and a plethora of other mammals that are after their honey. Despite their small size, bees are able to fend off even the largest of them due to their hive mentality. When working together, they can successfully defend the nest and the queen, but when they're away from the hive, a few lone bees won't be much of a match for an aggressor. Honey lures like a trap, Fedelma had said.

When I recalled those words, the buzzing ceased. I thought about what that might mean, and though the details of a plan were not clear to me, I knew the right thing to do was to bring Cerone to Hurstville.

The siblings still argued back and forth.

"Bernard is right," I said. I stood in the doorway and braced myself with the frame. I looked at Helen. "This community is not unlike your hives. You're stronger when you're here."

"She speaks some sense, then," Bernard said.

Stanley approached her. "I agree with the logic there, Helen. We are stronger here. We know this place and as of now the authorities have little interest in it. If we take it somewhere else, there's more of a chance the law will get involved."

And so it was decided. With only ten minutes to spare, a rudimentary plan was worked out. I called Cerone back, and a meeting was set up for four o'clock that afternoon. He would meet us in front of the limekilns and would bring Phinny with him.

I had to watch what I said, but I called Mama back and told her what was happening, that the man in the Farmer's Home was a gangster, and that he might have others with him. I asked her to close down the Farmer's Home for a while, go to my brother John's farm, and wait to hear from me. She was sure there was no one else at the hotel from the Chicago area. I assured her that there could just as easily be a carful of men parked outside keeping an eye on the place.

"If that's the case," she told me, "I don't need to be leading those men out to John's. I won't bring trouble any farther than it's come."

I admitted to the wisdom in that, and called in a favor from a fellow private investigator from Davenport to watch the hotel. I couldn't tell him exactly what was going on, but let him know that Mama was in real danger and he was to keep a close eye on her. It didn't make me feel completely comfortable, but when Mama had her mind set on something, there was nothing that could budge her.

"I'm sorry for causing you trouble," Mama said.

"It's okay, Mama. None of this is your fault."

"But it is."

"You couldn't have known he was someone to worry about. He could have found out the information he sought from a number of others."

"Like whom?"

"Like most of the people staying at the Farmer's Home. Like our neighbors. Most of those people know me, Mama."

"I suppose you're right, but that doesn't make me feel any better." Mama blew her nose.

A colony includes three kinds of bees: a queen, drones, and workers.

A queen comes into her role because she has emerged from gestation faster than the other potential queens and has killed her competition. Her queenship is not easy. Her primary job is to lay great quantities of eggs every day, a few thousand, in fact, and if she slows in her work, a new queen will take over. She is the mother of every bee in the hive and easy to spot for she is long and sleek, unlike her young. She also has another exceptional feature—a barbless stinger. Though it sounds less ruthless, the barbless feature allows her to sting an enemy multiple times because there's no barb to get caught in its flesh.

A drone is larger, like his queen, but where a queen's abdomen is pointed to allow for laying eggs in the small cells, a drone's abdomen is square and stocky. He also has large eyes that meet in the middle, all the better to spot a queen with. A drone doesn't mate with his own queen but with queens from other colonies. He has a lot of competition, so he needs to spot her early and use his speed and agility to get to her first. With no stinger, he isn't an effective hive guard. In fact, he has minimal work to do in the hive at all. He assists with some temperature control, shivering to generate heat or fanning to cool the hive down, but if he is taking too much food from the colony, especially during lean months, he will be kicked out to save food for the queen and her workers.

Workers might be small, but they're the most numerous bees in the hive. The life of a worker bee is much more complex since she will hold many jobs over her lifetime. At her youngest, a worker stays close to the brood, keeping the cells for developing bees warm and clean as the immature bees transition from eggs to larvae.

Once she has been alive for several days, the worker handles the nursing duties, which primarily means that she feeds the larvae a mixture she has regurgitated into the cells.

When a new group of nurse bees is ready for duty, the experienced worker moves on to building combs, secreting from her abdomen a wax which is then chewed and molded into hexagonal shapes so that it can house brood, honey stores, and pollen. She also manages the undertaking duties, hauling dead bees and depositing them outside the hive. Though her duties are many, she is allowed a considerable amount of time to rest in between tasks so she can store energy.

A worker eventually becomes a guard at the hive entrance, a transition into her remaining life as a forager, giving her a view of the world beyond the hive. Her duty as a guard is twofold. She will fan the hive to cool it down but also serves as an aggressor. Armed with a fully developed stinger packed with venom, she can defend the hive from predators. If she must sting a mammal, like a human or a mouse, she will surely die, for her barbed stinger will get stuck in the hard flesh and when she tries to fly, her insides will be strung out. If the invader is another bee or a wasp, she will survive the attack.

The last job a worker bee will have is that of forager, collecting nectar and pollen for the hungry hive. Her life span is largely determined by her mileage. Once her fragile wings are unable to fly, she dies.

In the Little Oklahoma side of Hurstville, Bernard and his men prepared the whiskey for exchange, 48 jars of honey whiskey, carefully packed to survive a long drive back to Chicago and stamped with "Wild River Honey." They drifted the shipment over via pontoon and loaded it onto a small wagon pulled by two grey mules. Bernard drove the wagon slowly while Raymond and Roy sat in back to secure the contents.

After the shipment was in place, Stanley gave the brothers another task. We had no real way of knowing whether Cerone would bring others, and in order to get something of a jump on the situation, Stanley sent Raymond and Roy to a bluff overlooking the road. If Cerone and Phinny were alone, they'd raise a green cloth, if there were more men coming, a red one. The two scrambled up the steep slope to wait.

School let out for the day and Stanley, Helen, and Marcus cleared most people from the downtown area and informed each household of the impending meeting. While they didn't go into the specifics of the exchange, it was made clear that it could get violent and all people, children especially, were to stay inside with the doors locked. Everyone in Hurstville knew how the town survived. No one gave any lip about it, although there were a couple of curious young boys who tried to hide underneath the post office porch. They gave themselves away when one let out a raucous sneeze. Helen grabbed their ears and walked them home.

The only people in town who stayed were those running the limestone furnaces. Two were ablaze that day and a warmth radiated from the sheds at the base of each furnace and out into the street. All remaining men were armed with the knowledge that the meeting could indeed go badly. They were to act as if nothing was amiss, to go about their jobs as usual, but to keep an eye on what was happening. If shooting started, they were backup. As we waited for the hour to arrive, each man retrieved a pistol or rifle which he stashed out of sight.

At the top of the limestone cliff, a mule hauled a cart filled with chunks of the yellow stone. While one man led the animal, two others walked along behind and began tossing large rocks down into a chimney stack. Though it was November, their blue work shirts were damp with perspiration and matted with lime. There were three more men in each of the two sheds working at cooling the powdered lime and packing it into barrels.

Walter and I waited on the café steps watching the activity. He was trying to get back into my good graces, although I hadn't taken the time to explain that he never was out of them. "Those furnaces burn so hot, even bones turn to ash," he said.

"How do you know that?" I asked.

"This past summer there was a rabid dog slobbering its way through the downtown. Someone shot it, and they threw the body into a furnace. The next day there wasn't a single trace of him left in there."

"I don't blame you for any of this, Walter."

He lowered his chin. "Maybe you should."

"That's ridiculous. I was on the case whether you were involved or not."

"Yeah, but until he saw us in the alley together, Cerone didn't know about you," Walter said.

"Whether I had a personal connection to you or not, I would have found you."

"Maybe."

"There is no maybe about it. I'm good at my job." I leaned over and playfully bumped his shoulder.

"I don't doubt that."

"Shut the hell up about it, then."

"Fair enough." Walter reached an arm around my shoulder and I rested my head on him.

"If something happens to Mama or Phinny, I'll never forgive myself."

"*You* don't start feeling guilty now."

"Especially Mama. If we all get out of this, I'm done living at the Farmer's Home. This won't happen again."

"This whole thing has me thinking about the future, too," Walter said.

Helen walked up to us then and asked me to join her. We walked a short distance away and left Walter sitting on the steps. "We've an hour or so to go. I want you to have something." She reached her hand into her coat pocket and drew out the pocket pistol I'd fired that morning.

"I can't take that."

"I have two more." Helen patted her other coat pocket and her left boot.

"I'm not comfortable—"

"Take the thing. If you don't need to use it today, then I'll take it back. If you find yourself in need, then you'll come around to wanting it." She left abruptly, not giving me any time to protest further. She joined Marcus who stood at the edge of town looking south toward Clinton.

They gazed into each other's eyes for a few seconds and stood so close I could have sworn they were lovers.

Bernard and Stanley stood just behind them, resting against the back of the wagon. Though they didn't look much like brothers, with Bernard's wild look and Stanley's neat one, their frames were nearly identical and they mirrored each other's postures, both standing with feet shoulder width apart and arms crossed.

The scheduled hour came and went as the fall sun sank behind the trees in the western sky, casting a shadow over Hurstville. The men continued to drop chunks of stone into the furnaces, each deposit resulting in a flaring of the fires that could be heard from inside the sheds.

It was past 4:30 when Raymond shouted from his position on the bluff. Roy waved a green cloth, and some of my concern diminished. At least Cerone and Phinny were alone.

The Ford coupe was incredibly muddy. Its white wheels were caked and had trouble gaining purchase over the short distance from the bluff to the downtown area. I assumed Cerone had underestimated the time it would take to cover Iowa's muddy roads, but when I saw Phinny at the wheel instead of Cerone, I wondered if Phinny's poor driving skills had contributed to the slow progress as well. He'd never quite gotten the hang of it. Whenever we went on a trip together, I begged Phinny to let me drive. Though he would never admit to being a bad driver, his persistent arthritic pain set his pride aside more often than not.

As the car approached, Walter and I joined Marcus and the three siblings in front of the wagon.

"Let me do the talking," Stanley said. "No one else says a goddamned thing." He looked sideways at Bernard and took a couple of steps forward.

Phinny stopped the car a good forty yards from where we stood and stepped out first. Cerone followed him out the driver's side door. He held his gun to Phinny's back while Phinny walked just ahead of him. The marks Mama told me about started alongside Cerone's left ear and ran down his neck, disappearing behind his white shirt collar.

Phinny's eyes were red-rimmed and bloodshot, his clothes wrinkled. His pants lacked the usual suspenders needed to hold them up, so he held them up with one hand. His coat hung loose and unbuttoned.

"You have what I asked for?" Cerone said.

Stanley cleared his throat and gestured toward the wagon behind him. "We have it."

Bernard shuffled his feet.

Cerone scanned the area, his eyes lighting on the men on the platform above. "This didn't have to be hard."

"I've no interest in making this any harder," Stanley said, "and I won't talk business while you're holding that gun."

"Fair enough." Cerone tucked his gun away and pushed Phinny ahead of him.

I stepped forward as Phinny stumbled, grabbing him by the arm before he could tumble.

"Are you all right?" I whispered.

"I'm fine, girl." Phinny grasped my hand, but there was a desperation in his hold that told me otherwise.

Introducing himself, Stanley explained that he took care of the business part of the operation. He then introduced Bernard and Helen, explaining that Bernard was in charge of distillation and Helen the honey production, respectively.

Bernard spoke up, "What is it you want exactly?"

Helen shot Bernard a look, but stayed quiet.

Cerone said, "Right now it's simple. You heard of Big Jim Colosimo?"

"We've heard of him," Stanley said.

I knew Colosimo had been the leader of the Chicago Outfit before he was murdered. The headline from the *Chicago Daily News* said, "Slaying of Colosimo Involved in Mystery of the Underworld." Phinny and I had been in Chicago at the time and the town was buzzing about it.

"How about Johnny Torrio?" Cerone asked.

"Can't say that I have," Bernard answered.

"He's in charge now," Cerone said, "and he's looking for some high quality whiskey—something special."

"I believe we have just the thing you're looking for," Stanley said.

"I think so, too, but that's for the boss to decide. I'm here to find quality and to check on the long-term prospects of your operation."

Above us, a mule pulling a rock cart began to make a fuss. The animal bucked, sending a shower of dust and rock below.

"I'm ready to get the hell out of here, but I need to see your setup first. Torrio expects a full report of the operation, so he can make a decision."

"It's not easy to get to," Bernard explained. "It's a walk and a boat ride from here."

"We'll do it now," Cerone barked. He glowered at me. "She'll come with us," he said. "Just her and you." He pointed at Bernard. "The rest of you'll stay here while we have a look. You can pile those crates into the car."

"I'll come too," Walter said.

"You'll stay here," Cerone barked at him. Cerone looked me up and down and grabbed my arm.

Walter clenched his fists. "You better not try a damn thing."

Cerone curled his upper lip. "Relax, lover boy."

Bernard broke in, "Sun's setting now. Let's get this over with."

"You have a weapon on you?" Cerone asked Bernard.

"You're welcome to check," he answered.

Cerone made a show of patting Bernard down, but Bernard showed no reaction. His beard hid any snarl he might have had.

I remembered I had Helen's gun, but Cerone made no move to check me for one. "Let's go," he said.

I gave a last look to Walter and Helen. Walter wouldn't look at me. Helen nodded and raised both eyebrows while she did so. I knew just what that look meant. I was to use the gun if need be.

Bernard brought a lantern with him, but we didn't need it until we reached the river. A deep chill set in and our breath shone in the light of the lamp as Bernard uncovered the motorized pontoon.

"Don't try anything stupid," Cerone said.

"Wouldn't dream of it," Bernard said.

"You first." Cerone touched my backside as he shoved me forward.

My temper flared as I'd a notion to reel around and knock him into next week. If he had felt just a few inches higher, he'd have noticed the gun I had stashed in the waist of my pants. My anger was doused by that relief.

Bernard read my reaction and grabbed hold of my arm, helping me onto the boat.

The pontoon had a short railing around all sides save the front. There were three wooden seats bolted to the floor, one in back near the motor and two others on the sides.

"Have a seat," Bernard said.

I did as he asked, but Cerone delayed. Instead, he bent at the waist and reached for the necklace Fedelma had given me. "What's this?" he asked.

"Don't touch it!" Resisting the urge to lash out, I bent back abruptly, causing the pontoon to rock. His hands were entirely too close to my neck, and Fedelma had taught me the nature of crystals. I knew Cerone could erase whatever protection she'd placed inside the jasper and though I wasn't sure I entirely believed in it, considering the circumstances, I wasn't taking any chances.

Cerone regained his balance easily enough and sat down. "Suit yourself."

When we reached the opposite side and began to disembark, I heard another craft being lowered into the water. Though Cerone didn't notice, I knew Walter was out there somewhere, keeping an eye on us. Given the state of his arm, I wondered who was managing the paddling.

Cerone had little to say during the tour of the distillery, just asked questions about quantity and how long it took the whiskey to age. He shed all appearance of scoundrel and focused on the business, much to my surprise. It was long after sundown when he was satisfied and we headed back to Hurstville.

"How'd you get away from the deputy, anyway?" I asked as we walked back through the woods of Little Oklahoma. Bernard's lantern threw dancing shadows through the bare trees.

"Wasn't hard," Cerone said. "Waited until the car was on the way and kicked him in the back of the head. Car veered off the road, hit a pole. Deputy was out cold. Got the keys off him and boom. Handcuffs off, gun back. I'm in business."

I decided to play to his ego a bit and continued. "We haven't seen the likes of Chicago gangsters yet."

Bernard worked up phlegm from his throat and spat.

"Even so, I'm surprised no one spotted you in Clinton the last few days," I said.

"I know how to blend in when I need to."

"You mentioned on the phone earlier that you have no choice but to see this through."

"That's right. The men I work for don't accept failure."

"Is that why you killed the Brownfields?"

"Something like that."

Bernard broke in. "Seems you had plenty of choice there."

"Guy was going for a gun under the counter."

"Seems Homer had a good reason to," Bernard said.

"All he had to do was give me some booze to take back home. If the bosses are pleased, we'll be back for more, I told him. Soon as he sniffed out Chicago, he didn't want a thing to do with it."

Bernard said, "Homer was no idiot. He knew all about what's going on in Chicago."

154

"He was trying to keep you and me from meeting," Cerone said. "Had his own pocket in mind. Probably afraid we'd wrestle distribution away from him."

"Was he wrong?" I asked.

"Right now, all they want is decent hooch in the city. Variety. Not the rotgut crap they've been selling."

"Right *now*," Bernard said, "but if Prohibition sticks, my guess is your people will reach further for distribution rights."

"That's not for me to say."

Bernard grunted.

"Why Rosela?" I asked.

"Because she was there," Cerone said, "and she pulled the same crap. 'Course Brownfield told me he was alone. Do all you Iowa seeds carry guns?"

"Not all of us," I said.

"Thought that was just a Chicago thing. 'Course she wasn't nearly as cute as you are to play with," Cerone said as he reached for me.

Bernard stepped between us. "That'll be enough of that."

Cerone held up his hands. "All right, all right." He smirked at me, his eyes twinkling devilish thoughts in the lamp light.

I couldn't bring myself to question him further about that night. I had many other unanswered questions but was afraid to push it with him. Cerone clearly had two minds. He could be businesslike one minute and a ruthless bastard the next. He had tried all night to get some information out of Rosela Brownfield. She held tight to what she knew.

Back in town, cattle lowed from the sheds near the railroad tracks and the sweet scent of manure hung in the cooling night air.

We emerged from the timber into the town center. Down the road, two pairs of bright headlights illuminated a small

155

crowd of people that had gathered there. Two trucks were parked just beside Cerone's. Stanley and Marcus faced five men dressed in white. They hid behind long robes and masks from which crude eyeholes had been cut. Stanley held a rifle at his side, as did each of the robed men. Helen and Phinny were nowhere in sight. I briefly wondered if she had taken him to rest in her home, but doubted Phinny would be able to take the long flight of stairs there. Walter was still hidden in the trees somewhere.

"What the hell is this?" Cerone asked.

"Trouble," Bernard said.

"The Klan?"

"They have no love of liquor and we have to pay to keep them quiet," Bernard said.

"There are easier ways to keep people quiet."

The three of us stopped just out of the light.

"You won't touch him," Stanley said to the men in white. "Marcus, you go home."

"Best you not move, nigger, if you want to survive the night," the Klan leader said. Unlike the plain white robes of the other four men, the front of his robe had at its center a red circle with a white equal-sided cross.

Stanley waved his left arm and three men from inside the cooling sheds walked out with rifles drawn. There was at least one man up above the chimneys, likely one or two more I couldn't see.

"Bad move, Kaufman. We'll shut you down faster than this nigger'll hang."

"Marcus didn't have a damn thing to do with that bank robbery, and you know it."

"I know no such thing. He's it as far as I'm concerned."

"What proof do you have?"

"He's a nigger, ain't he?"

156

Cerone had had enough waiting. He walked into the light with his revolver drawn at his side. "What kind of backwoods shit is this?"

Have you ever seen a cockfight? This was worse. Usually, there are just two in the ring, but imagine the chaos if there were more than you could count on your two hands.

One of the plain-robed men spoke. I recognized Cain's voice from the café. "Booze, niggers, and dagos, too? This is quite a show you got here."

Cerone picked up his pace. "What the hell did you just call me?"

Cain didn't answer him. "Where'd this dago come from, Stanley? You doing business with them now?"

Cerone's gun went off before anyone else got a word in. Cain immediately fell to the ground. Shouts ensued and more gunshots, but I didn't get a clear view of who was firing as Bernard grabbed my arm and we ran toward a cooling shed. Once inside, Bernard grabbed a rifle from a cupboard and approached the wagon entrance. From that open door, I saw Cain's body on the ground, a bloody plume spreading over his chest. Another Klansman was face down near him. The other three were positioned behind the vehicles, each with his own rifle. I couldn't see Stanley, Marcus, or Cerone but assumed they were still standing, for the three Klansmen were pointing their guns into the street.

"Stay here," Bernard said, and ran out the same door we came in.

"That's enough!" Stanley shouted.

"There's no stopping this now, Kaufman! Two of us are dead and two of you will answer for it!" The Klansmen each fired from their positions and that resulted in a volley of shots from the platform above. Two more Klansmen went down, but the leader ran straight for the cooling shed. He yanked his hood off and swung his head around looking for an exit. Instead of that exit, though, he found me instead.

Without realizing it, I had pulled Helen's pistol and the barrel of the gun was ten feet from his chest. It was like waking from a dream and finding myself standing outside, almost. Something instinctual had taken over.

With no time to raise his rifle, he stopped in his tracks and sneered. "What are you going to do with that, little lady?"

"Drop it," I said.

The Klansman's sneer reached up to his bulbous red nose. "That little stinger won't hurt me."

"Ten feet away and pointed right at your chest, you really want to take that chance?"

He lowered himself slowly and set the rifle on the ground. Rising back up, he lifted his hands into the air.

Behind him, Walter crept up slowly. He had taken his sling off but held his bad arm close to his body.

The man didn't hear him though because he kept running his mouth. "What are you doing with all these whiskey-making nigger-lovers? You're going to get yourself in some deep trouble if you don't look out."

"I'm doing just fine, mister, though I can't say the same for you," I said.

He licked his lips. "I'd like to lean you over my knee and . . ."

Walter didn't let him finish; he cracked his gun over the man's head, and he fell to the ground unconscious.

"He's the last one," Walter said.

"If he survived that crack, he is," I said. "You really conked him a good one. I didn't need you to do that, you know. I had it handled."

"I know you don't want saving, Elsie. It wasn't that. I knew what he was about to say, and I couldn't stand to hear him disrespect you."

It struck me that Walter was a might more observant than I had given him credit for. He was right. I didn't want saving. Instead of getting peeved at his actions, though, I was warmed by his sentiment.

I grabbed the man's rifle, and we reentered the light of the autos, though two of the headlights had been shot out.

Stanley and Marcus checked the bodies of the other four Klansmen. They were indeed dead.

"Hell of a mess," Stanley said.

Bernard and Helen walked down the set of stairs that led up to the chimney platform. Helen had Bernard's rifle in her hand. "Sure is. Not sure what's going to be harder to clean up. Those four or him," she said. Helen pointed the rifle at Cerone. His body was lying right where I'd last seen him. He had a bullet wound in the top of his head.

Though Cerone died that night, I was able to learn a little more about him thanks to Phinny. During Phinny's ordeal with Cerone over those trying days, Cerone had spilled details of his past.

Tino Cerone

I stood in a darkened corner, smoking a Cuban cigar given to me by Torrio himself. Six men sat around the mahogany table. Six more of us faded into the wall, all silent associates gunning for a seat at the table someday. With all the Bigs there, I sucked down my cigar like I was used to it and listened for an opportunity.

The newest round of profits was much more than anyone expected, so Torrio was feeling generous; the table was covered in pricey foods and a room full of women waited next door.

Capone became a full partner that night. Thanks to Prohibition, he worked his way up from a nothing in New York City to a big timer in Chicago. Even Torrio listened to him.

Though Torrio had Colosimo killed two years before, he realized Colosimo's desire to cater to the wealthy with high quality liquor wasn't such a bad idea.

Capone encouraged it. "Keep selling rotgut to the majority, but there's a market for premium," he said.

Bad liquor became the topic of their conversation. By the time the whiskey imported from Canada got to Chicago, the Purple Gang in Detroit had diluted it and added the devil knows what—the least of it, water, the worst of it, formaldehyde. The same could be said for the alky pouring in off the East Coast. It's time, they said, to find other sources of booze.

The men, including my boss, Sabella, talked for a long time about where to look, and it was decided that Iowa was the place to start. It wasn't far, just across the Mississippi River, and it smelled like opportunity. Unlike the rest of the nation, Prohibition had been in place there since 1916, so it was likely they had figured out how to meet demand. Covered in cornfields, they sure as hell had enough of the ingredients necessary to make something.

"We just need to see if they know what they're doing," Torrio said.

Capone spoke up. "There's no gang control just across the river either, so if we can find something special, we can control the price. It'll be easier than stripping the dresses off the girls in the next room."

Everyone laughed. We had learned to do that when Capone spoke. I laughed a little louder than everyone else, trying hard to get noticed.

Someone got out a map and laid it across the table. Capone's finger traced the river and found Dubuque, Clinton, Davenport, Muscatine, Burlington, and Fort Madison, all on the Iowa side. Each of the men at the table was given a city to sniff out. Sabella turned and looked at me, nodded his head.

They didn't do the sniffing themselves, of course. That work was left to the six of us.

"It's time to prove you're not just errand boys. See what you can find," Torrio ordered us. We were each assigned a city. For me, it was Clinton, probably the easiest to get to, right along the Lincoln Highway and a straight shot from Chicago. "You know what we're looking for. Pay a visit to every speakeasy in the city. When you find something worth barking about, track it down. If they don't want to sell it to us, you have my permission to bite. Let everyone know who's looking. If they're smart, they'll do business."

Capone had been ignoring the ashes building up on his cigar and they fell on the map. He blew them away with his fat lips and grinned. "There's nowhere to go but up, boys."

Elsie Edens
Friday, November 10, 1922

Nothing so needs reforming as other people's habits. Fanatics will never learn that, though it be written in letters of gold across the sky. It is the prohibition that makes anything precious.
—Mark Twain

Human remains are cremated at 1100 degrees. Don't ask me how I know that.

The limestone furnaces in Hurstville burned at 1700 degrees. I can't say for sure what the Kaufmans did with the bodies, but suffice it to say there were no signs of them the next day. The furnaces burned throughout the night; the smoke from them rose above the trees and could be seen in the light of the waning moon from my window at Helen's house.

Morality is a funny thing. It changes as one gets older. What once seemed out of the question becomes tolerable, becomes understandable, becomes necessary for survival. I used to trust the police and the government. I lost my trust in the law after my sister died. That's when I learned sometimes people have to take matters into their own hands for the good of the people. The government's resistance to a woman's right to vote as well as the entire fiasco of

Prohibition had erased my respect for the government. What do we all really have when it comes down to it? No one but ourselves, really, and our own moral compass to guide us. I can pick and choose cases as I see fit and deal with them as I see fit. To dig, to hide, to cover, to reveal, to probe, to conjure, to restore, to justify, to validate, to save, to kill. All of these things I choose myself. That's where I am now, anyway. Who's to say I won't change? Maybe when I'm retired I'll look back at all these things and be appalled at what I did. Maybe not.

The Klansman who survived the firefight was held in the post office, a makeshift jail a part of its construction in anticipation of the occasional drunkard who needed to sleep it off. Marcus and a couple of other men volunteered to take shifts watching over him while the Kaufman siblings decided what to do next. It was an easy job, for the man was still passed out cold nearly 24 hours later.

"You can see how bad I am now," Phinny said, "why I don't go out."

Phinny and I sat in Helen's kitchen and sipped hot tea. Helen had brewed him a special concoction meant to help his aches and pains.

"I see it; I've known. I just haven't said anything."

"I want you to take over the business. My mind doesn't want to be done, but the pain is too much to bear any more."

"I understand, Phinny. I'm ready." In an attempt to lighten the mood, I added, "I'll take the business, but I won't take the damn bird." It just came out. I'd forgotten I hadn't heard C. Auguste Dupin when I'd called him. Likely as not, Cerone had killed the thing. I'd certainly had the desire to do so more than once.

"That won't be necessary."

"What do you mean?" That's it then, I thought, I'd stuck my foot in it. Phinny had loved that damn bird.

"I'm moving, Elsie. Albuquerque's weather will help my aches and pains. I won't be taking him."

I feigned concern. "What happened to it?"

"I walked him over to Mave's. Thought she'd appreciate his sass."

"So the bird's fine then? I thought maybe . . ." I set my cup down, unwilling to explain what I had thought.

"Hate to disappoint you, but Dupin is alive and well," Phinny said. Phinny read me just as well as Mama.

"What'd Mave think?" I asked.

"She mentioned something about Louise needing a friend. Guess she was going to give Dupin to her to take care of."

I wished I had thought of that. A companion was exactly what Louise needed.

"I'll worry about you," Phinny said.

"Why?"

"I can see you changing before me. You're not so young and innocent. You're only—"

"Twenty-two and I haven't been innocent for a long time. Long before I started this job, anyway." I stood and reached for the pot of warm water, busying myself at the counter.

"The boy, Walter—he's the one who found your sister's body, isn't he?"

"He's the one."

"You know, you never told me what really happened to her."

"What do you mean?"

"You forgot what my job is? Anyone who reads the papers could see it was a cover-up. She didn't kill herself."

"I don't really want to talk about it."

"Has it ever occurred to you that if you told someone about your secrets you'd feel a hell of a lot better? I have a few of my own, you know. They used to haunt every footstep I took until I got rid of them."

"I'm used to ghosts," I said.

"You shouldn't be."

"I wouldn't be the same person without them."

I had watched the blood from Minnie's killer soak through the rug and filter down into the floorboards. Traces of his blood are still there. How can they not be? The boards hold onto those traces and they haunt the steps of everyone who crosses over.

But there were darker traces in my past. Somewhere in that Minneapolis alley there were flecks of old pains and old dyings. Hester Tate's murderer deserved to die, of that I had no doubt, but that didn't change the fact that his ghost loomed over my shoulder.

"Whatever it is, it's a hard secret to hold onto for such a young person," Phinny said.

Pretending we were just talking about Minnie's killer, I said, "It was a long time ago."

"Yes, but it stays with you, doesn't it?"

Though Cerone and several other men were dead, the trouble was far from over. We had no way of knowing whether Cerone or the Klansmen had told others where they were going. All hoped, however, that we at least had some breathing room before needing to be on high alert.

Phinny's ordeal with Cerone had him feeling even more sore and symptomatic than usual. Helen tended to him with as much tender loving care as he would allow, though Phinny's favorite part of the treatment was a healthy dose of honey whiskey every few hours. Neither Phinny nor I had any desire to head back to Clinton with so much unresolved business. Though the man who shot Homer and Rosela Brownfield was dead, those behind his actions certainly were not, and in all probability, they would find us before we found them. Phinny stuck close to Helen's fire and remained quiet and pensive all day and into the night.

Helen, Alice, and several of the other ladies in town served a feast that Friday evening: roast chicken, biscuits with butter and honey, green beans, mashed potatoes and gravy, apple pie, and an assortment of other foods. The community joined together at Alice's café where three men I recognized from the limekilns played lively music on string instruments and sipped whiskey between songs.

Walter joined some of the men outside for a cigarette. That bad habit was one I was determined to avoid. I stood by myself for a moment before Bernard walked up to me and raised his chin in Helen's direction. She stood with Marcus and laughed at something he said. "You know she's the queen bee around here, right?"

"I figured that," I said, smiling.

"I wouldn't admit that to her, though."

"I understand," I said.

"You mind stepping outside?" Bernard asked.

The door shut behind us and the music faded into the background.

Walter and the men had walked over to the kiln site and discussed something in low tones.

"She likes you," he told me.

"I'm glad to hear it. How about you?" I asked.

"I'm still deciding." Bernard took out a corncob pipe, and packed it with sweet smelling tobacco. Coyotes yipped and howled somewhere in the dark across the railroad tracks. "Before the white man was here, this whole area was packed with Sac and Fox Indians." Bernard swept his hand around, indicating the areas up and down both sides of the river. "They say those coyotes are the spirits of the dead roaming the land." He lit his pipe.

"I like that," I said.

"We're not unlike the Indians, you know."

"How do you mean?"

"Hurstville will fade someday just as they did. Just over there," Bernard pointed into the west, toward the howling coyotes, "was their dancing ground. Pretty overgrown now but it's circled by old cedars and hugged by the slough. Can still see some traces of the path leading to it."

"Do you ever find arrowheads around here?"

"All kinds of things. Arrowheads, bits of pottery, stone pipes, war clubs. Several mounds west of here, too."

"Mounds?"

"The Sac and Fox built up mounds of dirt in the shapes of bear or bird, other animals, too."

"Why?"

"No one knows for sure, but I think they acted as some kind of territory marker, a sign for other tribes."

"What happened to them?"

"Before the Civil War most of 'em died of smallpox. They're buried on the Sand Ridge in the forks, close to here."

I remembered Minnie talking about the natives she saw coming through the Elvira area years ago. They dragged shaggy ponies and traded in furs, hanging onto an old way of life by their fingernails.

It could have been the whiskey. It could have been, but I swear I saw figures dancing in the light of the waning moon—just beyond the tracks, mingling with the sound of the coyotes.

Before Prohibition, the federal government was pulling more than seventy percent of its internal revenue from alcohol sales. This fact made it the number one obstacle in the passing of the Eighteenth amendment. People wondered, how was the government to fill that enormous gap?

Enter income tax.

Though demands for Prohibition reached back into the 1800s, it didn't gain much ground until income tax became a permanent part of the tax system in 1913. Problem solved.

The Woman's Christian Temperance Union, the Anti-Saloon League, other temperance organizations, the KKK, and The Great War all added to a stew that made the Prohibition amendment politically possible. The desire for temperance made for some strange bedfellows.

The first recorded arrest made under the new Prohibition laws happened in Peoria, Illinois, the self-proclaimed whiskey capital of the United States. The arrested men weren't gangsters, however, but distillers who were attempting to haul off a couple truckloads of their own whiskey. Who can blame them?

The amendment didn't stop alcohol consumption, it simply shifted the income from one set of hands to another. Until 1920, gangs from different cities had no reason to play nice with each other. Once Prohibition took effect, gangsters quickly took a bite out of the financial opportunity, and it didn't take long for them to begin working together out of necessity. This necessity birthed organized crime as we know it. Liquor needed to cross state lines, forcing enemies to become friends. Once a partnership was established between two areas, the mob expected a piece of everything in between. Mob influence flooded what was once an artisan market. In the early years of Prohibition, the best local alcohol went for as much as $20 a gallon. In the later years, a jug of moonshine ran around $5. Once the mob came in, they took control, beefed up production, usually watered down the quality, and made it all about profit.

No one had heard of dinner parties before Prohibition, but there were sure a lot of them once it came into effect. People gathered for supper, but that wasn't the main attraction. With plenty of bootleg alcohol, folks danced and ate, flirted and cajoled, and simply enjoyed the world they had built for themselves.

The party at Alice's reached far into the evening hours. The music continued, but the three musicians toned down the party atmosphere with a rendition of "Some of These Days" by Sophie Tucker. Though no one sang the words, I remembered them from Minnie's old records: "I feel so lonely, just for you only, for you know, honey, you've had your way." Couples regathered on the makeshift dance floor created by shoving tables and chairs to the corners of the room. Helen danced with Marcus and no one seemed to notice or care. Stanley and Bernard stood with a group of single men near the kitchen. Alice was trying to clean up a spill but was hauled to the dance floor by a gentleman who made her laugh.

Raymond and Roy wiped tables and refilled glasses, Raymond clearly enjoying himself as he joked with the guests.

Walter and I stood together, watching the couples. I'd a strong urge to join the dancers, but an idiotic attachment to protocol wouldn't allow me to ask him. Besides, the exertion from the night before caused Walter's arm to pain him. He didn't say so, but winced with every movement. When I'd checked it the night before, there were no signs of infection. Fedelma's advice held true.

I sipped too much whiskey, much too much for a lady anyway, not that I ever was one. Walter seemed to read my mind and took my hand, despite his discomfort. We walked out onto the floor. With his bad arm back in a sling, it was impossible to dance in the traditional way, so I reached both arms up to his shoulders and Walter's good hand slid to the small of my back while his sling remained the only barrier between us. I would never have danced in such a way back home, but there was an air of to-hell-with-it that night. He smelled of Brilliantine that tamed and slicked back his hair and sweet honey whiskey, an intoxicating mixture which had me thinking . . . well, never mind that.

Some of the couples began to disperse before the midnight hour. The door opened and closed often, so I didn't notice a group of four strangers enter the building until one of the men shouted over the music, "Sorry to disturb your party, but anyone know where I can find the man who makes this?" He held up a jar of the honey whiskey; its tag blew in the breeze of the closing door. The man wore a dark grey suit, black bow tie, and a grey hat tipped with a black ribbon. He was the tallest of the four men, and had kind and slightly baggy eyes. When he shifted his weight to one side, he placed his hand on his waist, moving his jacket ever so slightly and revealing a hefty revolver. The other men all flanked him and scanned the crowd.

Not wanting to give Bernard up, every person in the place kept his or her eyes on the four men instead of looking at him. The music stopped, and the musicians packed up and called it a night. With glances at their husbands, most of the women also departed. Walter and I left the dance floor and took a spot behind the counter with Alice, as did Helen and Marcus, Raymond and Roy.

"Someone going to say something?" the man asked.

Bernard didn't move, but said, "Who the hell are you?"

"It's not so important who I am," he said, "but who I represent."

"And who might that be?" Bernard replied.

"You met Tino Cerone by now, I assume."

Stanley spoke up then. "We have."

"And where might he be?" the man asked.

"That's a long story," Stanley said.

"It might be late, but I think I need to hear that story. We're here to do business, not cause trouble."

Stanley asked us to leave—Walter and me, Helen and Marcus, Alice, the boys, and the remaining men. No one moved.

Helen spoke up. "We're not going anywhere."

Stanley didn't push it further but mumbled something to Bernard.

Bernard turned to me and said, "I think you're the best one to explain what led to the current state of things since you're not on either side. How about you start with the Brownfields?"

He caught me off guard. I stammered a bit but realized the wisdom in that decision. I introduced myself first, as a private investigator hired to look into the deaths of the couple. I started with the crime at the Brownfield store and led him right up to the gunfight that had taken place with the Klan the night before. The only part I really fudged was the part where I said a Klansman had killed Cerone. It could have been anyone, really, but given the angle of the bullet and that fact that she had been on the chimney platform, I strongly suspected Helen of the deed.

Although none of us could prove who had actually shot Cerone, the fact that one of the Klansman was still alive and being held in the jail added some credibility to the story. The man, who introduced himself as Carmine Sabella, asked to see the prisoner, and we all walked the short distance through town to the post office where he was held. The head of the man who guarded him rose abruptly when we walked in, eyes bloodshot; he'd clearly been sleeping. His prone charge was barely conscious and behind a heavy set of bars.

Klan robe still on and his hood tossed to the floor, the Klansman mumbled, "This won't stand. The Klan will bring you all down. This won't stand. You're all going to die just like that wop."

That was all the proof he needed, apparently, for Sabella nodded to Bernard and Stanley, and we left the building.

"I apologize for the ill treatment of the Brownfields. Cerone was a hothead. Known for unwise decisions. What's done can't be undone, but the fact remains that the boss wants what you have to sell. We're prepared to talk business and sweeten the pot in compensation for your lost revenue. I understand Brownfield was a major distributor?"

"That's right," Stanley said.

Sabella said, "We'll make up for that a hundredfold."

Tino Cerone

A little money bought me the information I was looking for at a cathouse on Second Street in Clinton. I walked out with three addresses in the downtown area, all of which supposedly had decent hooch.

The first place was a greasy room in the back of a small garage. A scruffy mutt guarded the back door from the outside; his growl let the doorman know I was there. He couldn't have been too concerned about the police because he opened the door wide. "Don't know who you are, but you don't look like the law," he said.

"I'm not," I replied. "Just thirsty." That's really all it took, much different than the passwords and secret doors in Chicago. What they had wasn't bad. Mostly home brew beer and bathtub gin, but at least it wasn't mixed with embalming fluid.

Next I went to an old rail car that sat behind some abandoned warehouses. Surrounded by old trees and wrapped with vines, it was fairly hidden. Men off work from the lumberyards and factories paid for jars of sweet wine and

moonshine from two men in overalls. Not what Torrio was looking for.

The last address was a long, narrow joint in the back of a downtown café. A sassy redhead ran the place and took a shine to me. I can be charming when I want to be. I asked her to serve me her best. Her best was something all right, the likes of which we needed more of in the city. It wasn't moonshine. It was whiskey. Fine whiskey. Someone knew what he was doing. She said she didn't know where it came from, but that it was delivered to her at six on Friday mornings. I smiled and downed the rest of my glass.

I walked into the alleyway in back of the café just before six a.m.; there was no one else around. The streets were quiet until a truck drove in. Its lights were on in the early morning light, but I was hidden in a doorway on the opposite side.

The delivery driver was no more than a kid. Maybe seventeen, eighteen. I didn't let him know I was there until he unloaded the crates, six of them stacked neatly inside the back door of the place. Ten more stayed in the bed of the truck.

He was reluctant to give up any information, but twenty bucks bought me a meeting and a sample to send back to Chicago.

"Meet me here at nine tonight," he said. "I'll see what I can do."

Later that night, I sat in my car waiting for the kid to show. He pulled up right beside me and shouted over the cranking of his engine, "Follow me!" I didn't expect to be leaving town, but we exited the city and hit the complete dark of the countryside. Nearly ten miles out, we finally pulled into the lot of a simple country store. A little dog ran around from the back and jumped up on the kid.

"I'm going to introduce you to Mr. Brownfield. There's a certain way he likes to do things. He'll be the one to decide whether he wants to do business with you or not," the kid said.

It was late, so the place was locked up, but the front light was still on when he knocked on the screen door. I could see the storekeeper wrapping packages at the counter. He took slow, heavy steps over to the door and looked out at us.

"I know it's after closing time, Mr. Brownfield, but this man is hoping to talk anyway," the kid said.

"Just need a little refreshment," I said. "Been on the road since Chicago, and I've a powerful thirst. Won't take much of your time."

The man looked at me long and hard, then checked out my car. He took a deep breath and unlatched the door. Funny how the littlest of decisions can decide your fate, and you never know what that little thing might be. Could be something as small as deciding to leave from your house five minutes earlier, and that's the one moment that's necessary to meet the oncoming car at the corner of Main and Sutton that'll make meat out of you. All of this world's just shit and dumb luck. And don't let anyone tell you otherwise. If they do, they're just a fool.

"What can I do for you?" he asked.

"I represent interests in Chicago. We're on the lookout for quality whiskey. I found some at a place along the river and that led me to the kid," I said.

"Is that right?" The guy was a good foot taller than me and didn't bother to hide the gun tucked into a holster at his side. His shirtsleeves were rolled up, vest unbuttoned. He walked around behind the counter. "It's time for you to call it a night," he said to the kid.

The kid nodded to me and took off.

"I know you have quantity. I saw it in the back of the kid's truck this morning," I said. "I just need about that amount to head east. I'm prepared to buy a shipment immediately. If the bosses are pleased, we'll be back for more."

"Bosses?"

"Let's just say, if you make us happy, there'll be a lot of money heading your way."

"The people I deal with aren't set up to be dealing with large quantities. It's a small operation."

"Small operations can grow," I said.

"They're families, just trying to get by, and they're doing just fine without Chicago."

"Let them say whether they're doing just fine or not. Once they see the numbers we're talking, I have a feeling they'll be convinced to step up production."

"I don't think so," he said.

"You set up a meeting, and we'll let them decide."

"I'm not looking to get mixed up with Chicago."

"No mixing necessary, just straight whiskey."

"And if I refuse?"

"That really wouldn't be wise. You can either be part of the deal or part of the problem. I'm sure you're not the only one who knows where it comes from."

"No one knows a damn thing about it except me. I've made sure to keep it that way," he said.

"I doubt that."

"The boy doesn't know where the whiskey comes from. That's not his job. He delivers from the store to local spots only." At that point, I saw the man glance at the back of the store.

"Anyone else here?"

"No."

"You sure about that?"

"There's no one else here." He looked me dead in the eye when he said it.

I had a feeling he was past the point of persuasion, so I opened my jacket, revealing my gun. "One way or another we'll get to it."

The next thing I know he's offering me up a cup of ice cream. Ice cream. He bends over and gets out a scoop before I say, "I don't want that shit; I want information." I eyed that revolver at his side and decided to play it safe. Aiming my gun at his chest, I warned, "Back away from the counter and raise your hands away from that gun of yours."

But the bastard didn't listen, and he acted like he was going in for another scoop. I saw him twitch a bit, like he was reaching down deeper than before. I felt sure he was going for a gun and not the one he had on him. I blasted him right then and there, while he was still bent over. Tall bastard, but he wasn't so tall slumped down on the floor.

I heard a floorboard groan in one of the back rooms, so I ran back to check it out. Turns out a woman was back there. Soon as I entered the room, she dropped a sack of flour, busting it all over the floor. She let out a scream and tried to reach for the window before I whacked her over the head with the butt of my gun and down she went.

Man dead, woman passed out, the trail was dead unless I found the kid again or could figure out where Brownfield was getting the whiskey. I knew those two weren't the distillers, only the means to some information. The best thing was to go right to the source anyway. I went out to the porch and shut off the lamp light so as to turn away any late-night guests. Two other lamps hung inside the store, and I needed the light but didn't want to be seen from the road, so I shut one off and turned the other down low.

Looking for a pattern of names, places, dates, I began to go through the register and bankbooks. I found the man's pocketbook and went through that, too. There wasn't a thing to be found as far as I could see. No record of any money

consistently going out to a particular name, not a damn thing. While going through the paperwork, I heard a shuffle coming from her. The woman crawled out from the storeroom door. She scrambled for the other back room where there was an outside door. She managed to push it open just enough to let the dog in before I ran at her, sending her spinning off up the stairs instead. The dog let out a yelp, but didn't follow us up the stairs, just high-tailed it into the main room.

It took all night just to get a little something from her. "Jackson County. Backwoods." I could figure out how to find Jackson County, but "backwoods" wasn't enough. I didn't know for sure, but I imagined the kid probably had a good idea where it came from. I knew I had to track him down again.

I had no intentions of killing her and was sure she knew nothing more, so I decided to gather some things I'd pilfered through and burn them. Fingerprints could be used to track me down eventually—unlikely, but possible. So I took the bankbook, wallet, and papers, set them on fire in the backyard and wiped down anything else I touched. By that time the sun was coming up. I thought about dragging her out and torching the place, but I decided that seeing the man slumped behind the counter with a bullet to his head would be a decent deterrent to further bullshit. He needed to be seen. People around there needed to know they were messing with the big-times.

When I came in that back door, there she was again—standing, bloody, half-dressed. I couldn't believe she was awake, let alone standing. That time she had a gun, a small one. I shot her before she worked up the nerve. She had a chance. It's not my fault she threw it away.

As I drove away, the rain started, but by that time the store hours meant customers, so I hoped the fire burning in the backyard had done its job.

I hate to admit this, but, hell, who's listening? It happens sometimes when I'm walking down a quiet street in the dark or slinking back into the scene of a crime. I hear footsteps, breathing, or whispers, and I know they are the reflection of the dead. Since they haunt my steps, you'd think I'd change, wouldn't you? But somehow, it only makes me more of who I already am.

Elsie Edens
Saturday, November 11, 1922

What makes night within us may leave stars.
—Victor Hugo

I sat at Helen's kitchen table drinking coffee and making notes on the last few days. A small grey mouse scurried back and forth from a pile of crumbs near the butter churn to a hole in the wall underneath the sink. Eager for time alone, I had walked down without changing or doing my hair. My brown locks trailed down my back and the chill of the wooden floorboards reached itself up into my nightgown. When Helen, Walter, Phinny, and I talked into the late evening hours the night before, Walter had fallen asleep on Helen's couch. Helen didn't have the heart to force him back to Stanley's place, so she ushered him up the stairs to another spare room, where he still slept. On my way down to the kitchen, I heard his soft breathing coming from the room next to mine and peered in. People look like such angels when they sleep. Walter was no exception. Normally tamed by wax, his hair took on its natural curl in the night, and fell over one of his eyes. His good arm rested on his forehead and his biceps clenched while he dreamed.

The mystery of who killed Homer and Rosela was solved, though the fact that justice was served couldn't be told to either the authorities or the woman who hired us. Cerone was dead, but as far as anyone else knew, he was on the lam and far from Iowa.

I pretended not to notice Marcus come down the staircase and sneak out the back door. His shirttail was askew and the left leg of his pants was caught in his sock. He didn't see me though he must have smelled the coffee brewing.

Still in her robe, Helen followed him down moments later and watched him walk across the back lawn. Like fragile armor, the frost clung to the grass, causing Marcus's footsteps to crunch all the way home. "We love who we love," she said.

"That's the truth of it." I poured Helen a cup of coffee.

"I know who loves you," she said.

I played dumb, though as soon as she said it, I knew.

"He can't keep his eyes off you. Haven't you noticed?"

My underarms broke out in a sweat, though inside I blamed that on the heat from the coffee and not embarrassment. I excused myself from the table, making a lame attempt at an explanation. "It's important we get on the road early today," I said. "I should clean up." I hadn't even given a thought to the fact that my vehicle was still in the ditch.

"Don't close your mind to him," she said. "He may be young, but he's already a good man."

Helen didn't understand. Men weren't on my priority list. I saw myself existing on the cusp of a great tidal wave of change, and I'd every mind to be a part of it. I questioned everything traditional—marriage, concepts of good and evil, the church, women's roles. I looked to science and all things literary. I hung up the chains of everything that bound me and found my own road, one I sniffed out, hacked away, loved, cajoled, slapped, and kissed into being. It was either that or die trying.

Even so, Walter wasn't my first. A beautiful, tall boy from Madison was. I don't know if I was Walter's first or not. We never talked about it. People didn't talk about those things back then. It didn't matter, anyway.

Reaching back to our childhood, we had a trust deeper than the roots of the maple tree, sunk deep among the limestone caverns dripping with water, magical and earthen beyond the concept of time. We both knew there was nothing that could outdo it.

A soft, pink light reached out from underneath the door of the second floor washroom. It was quiet, so I knocked. Walter called to me. A small splashing of water. I walked in, and then he emerged from a tub, towel wrapped around his waist like a god made just for me. I walked in and closed the door.

There was something about that place that made me want to stay. It was an old way of life, a simple one. It was biscuits on the counter in the morning. It was honeybees. Hot toddies for pain. Acceptance. All simple truths.

Helen and I sat on her front step waiting for Phinny and Walter. Our stay had come to an end. I held a jar of Wild River Honey in my hand.

"You'll keep the gun," Helen said.

"I didn't really use it." The pocket pistol was still in my coat. I'd forgotten it was there.

"Walter told me what happened in there. Who knows what you might have done if he hadn't knocked him out." She was right. Even I didn't know what I would have done.

"I've no need of it. I have others," Helen said.

"What are you afraid of?" I asked.

Helen tapped her apron pocket. "Thanks to this, I'm not afraid of a damn thing."

I nodded my head. Helen was a hard nut. I liked her that way.

Phinny's footsteps sounded on the creaky stairs. He plodded his way down and joined us, thanking Helen for her hospitality.

"I've something for you, too, Mr. Lawrence." Helen went back inside and came out with a crate. "This ought to keep your arthritis in check. Honey whiskey and the tea you've been drinking. Keep up with it."

"Gladly," Phinny said.

Marcus arrived and informed us that Walter waited near Alice's with my marooned car. Men from town had used a tractor to haul it out in the early morning hours. Marcus took the crate from Helen and walked us down to it.

Raymond and Roy were polishing my windows as we descended the stairs into Hurstville. Walter talked with Alice just outside her front door.

"Your chariot, Miss Elsie." Raymond raised his rag in the air and twirled it downward with a flourish.

The car must have been completely covered in mud and muck, but gleamed with their efforts. I thanked them.

Walter and Raymond exchanged handshakes and patted each other on the back.

"Be seeing you around?" Raymond asked.

"Most likely," Walter said.

Stanley and Bernard came out of the shed where Stanley kept his office.

Bernard said to the brothers, "If you're done here, get back to the stills. Time to clean the vats."

Raymond and Roy each tipped their hats to me and left.

"Is it okay?" I asked Stanley.

"Won't hurt anything," he said.

"What are you two talking about?" Walter asked.

"Before we say goodbye, I've something quick I need to do," I said. "Come with me." I pulled on Walter's coat sleeve.

I led him over to the kilns and up the stairs. Men had finished adding a wagonload of rock into one and led a mule back off the platform. We waited for them to pass and I walked Walter over to the mouth of the chimney. The fire raged below and warmed our faces in the November chill. Its orange light played off the inside of the stack.

"What are we doing here?" Walter asked.

"We're going to take care of something," I said. I pulled the Brownfields' logbook from my coat and showed it to him.

"What's that?"

"The only record of your mother's debt."

"Really?"

"As far as I know, yes."

"And what are we doing here?"

"We're getting rid of it." I flung the book down into the chimney.

Walter's eyes followed its descent. "Thank you, Elsie."

I smiled up at him and Walter gave me a hug, then kissed me square on the lips. I wondered if any of them saw us, but realized I didn't really care. Straightening my hat and coat I said, "We ought to go. Phinny's waiting."

Despite the bumpy ride, Phinny had somehow fallen asleep and snored between us. His head lolled forward.

I drove to Elvira to drop Walter off at his mother's house before heading back to the office.

Two men were on the roof of his home pounding on new shingles.

His younger sister sat on the porch petting a little dog. The brown and white terrier looked familiar.

"You recognize the dog?" Walter asked.

"Is that—"

"Mr. Brownfield's terrier. When I went back to take the whiskey from the basement that night, I found him crouched under the porch."

"Poor thing."

"He's not so poor now." The dog rolled on his back, exposing his belly to a good rub.

"Speaking of whiskey, where did you stash the shipment that was in the Brownfield store?"

Before he could answer, his sister ran down the stairs. Her dress looked so new the fabric was stiff. "Howdy, Walter. Is that your girlfriend?"

"This is my *friend*, Elsie. Don't be so nosy."

Phinny woke and stared blankly ahead.

"Mama's been worried about you," the little girl said. She was maybe ten and wore her hair in double braids.

"No need for that. Here I am."

The terrier yapped at her, and she turned and chased it around the house.

New roof, new dress. Walter had unloaded the shipment and given the money to his mother.

He grasped the door handle, but before he could open it, I said, "I won't try to change you, Walter, but I wish you'd find a job that's not so dangerous. There's even more reason to worry now that Chicago is involved."

"My job isn't the only one that's risky. What about yours?"

My mind flashed back to that Minneapolis alley; then I remembered Helen's pistol. My pistol.

"I can take care of myself."

"And so can I," Walter said.

"Elsie could use some assistance. I'm getting out of Iowa, you know," Phinny said.

Walter didn't respond, just opened the door and said, "I'll see you soon."

I liked the idea of Walter being close. The rest of the way home I imagined a future like that.

Elsie Edens
Sometime Later

Truth is so rare; it is delightful to tell it.
—Emily Dickinson

A few weeks after this whole mess was wrapped up, I brought a spider plant over to Mave's to give to Louise. I thought she might appreciate a substitute for the yucca that was killed when she knocked out Tino Cerone but couldn't manage to find an exact replacement anywhere. The large yucca was her pride and joy, and the fact that she used it to protect Walter and me spoke of her general good nature despite what people said about her. A little bit of me was also curious about how Louise and C. Auguste Dupin were getting along.

Nathan and Mave had checked on Louise when the dust settled in the alley that night. Not wanting to bring Louise into a police investigation, nothing was said about her role in knocking out Tino Cerone with a houseplant. When they went into her apartment she was hiding in the closet with the lights off, knees up to her chest.

Nathan assured her she did a good thing and Mave tried to coax her out. They both assumed Louise was afraid she would get in trouble for her actions, but that wasn't what she was afraid of.

"He got away," she told them.

"Who?" they asked.

"The bad man. He got away. Driving his car." She pointed out the front window toward the street.

Nathan assured her, "I won't let anyone hurt you, Louise. I'm not going anywhere."

Mave had to get stern with Louise to get her out of the closet. She had a job to do, Mave told her, and her job was the most important one of all. None of them got a wink of sleep that night. Nathan watched the back door, Mave watched the front, and Louise was back to her station on the top floor, watching everything.

Louise and C. Auguste Dupin were both perched near the window when I walked into her room.

Dupin let out a single bark, then said, "He got away."

"Who got away?" I asked Louise, knowing they were her words the bird was repeating.

"The man who tried to kill you." Louise stroked Dupin's feathers as he preened.

"Louise," I said, "You don't have to worry about that."

"I don't want you to die. I don't want to die."

"Louise, if I tell you something, do you promise not to tell anyone?"

She perked up. I had forgotten how alarming her bright blue eyes were.

"That man can't hurt anybody anymore. He's dead."

"He is?"

"Absolutely, unequivocally dead, yes."

"He's dead?"

"Yes, but it might be best if you keep saying that he got away. We don't want Dupin to give it away. It's a secret."

"I can keep secrets," Louise said. She placed her pointer finger up to her lips and said, "He got away."

Dupin mimicked her again and ruffled his feathers.

Since Tino Cerone escaped, there was no legal closure to the case, causing all sorts of speculation and rumor. Two years after these events, a young man by the name of Harold Dannatt came forward and confessed to the murders, implicating two other young men as well. Days later he recanted his statement explaining that he was the only one involved. Dannatt, who had a reputation for being unbalanced due to poisonous bootleg alcohol and a kick in the head he received from a horse as a child, was found to be mentally unstable. His claims were dismissed.

In 1925, two men actually went to trial over the whole thing. The rumrunners from Cedar Rapids, Dan O'Neal and Buck McLaughlin, were known to transport booze from Chicago. Authorities arrested O'Neal, a colored fellow, on a tip from one Effie Wilson. His supposed counterpart was already in jail for robbery and housed at the Kansas State Penitentiary. Effie Wilson's information was supported by Clara W., who had heard what could have been a gunshot as she drove by the Brownfield store and reported seeing a colored man speeding away from the scene of the crime. The case fell apart when numerous people came forward and vouched for O'Neal's whereabouts. Effie Wilson was charged with perjury when it became clear she lied about O'Neal's involvement. Though McLaughlin wasn't exonerated in the light of the new information, the case against him ceased. A local detective agency may have had something to do with that, but I'll never tell.

Though I knew who killed them, the crime scene at the Brownfields' store occupied my thoughts. I tried to piece

things together, moment by moment. It had to make sense in my mind.

My sister's crime scene still plagued me even after all those years. Though it was morbid beyond belief, I needed to see the action of that night. The clues had to piece together into a logical puzzle. I imagined Sherlock Holmes coming to life, puffing his pipe, and mapping it all out for me. She was found hanged in her barn. With the area completely covered in mud, there was no way for Minnie to get from the house to the barn without getting filthy. When she was found, her stockings and floor length nightgown were completely clean. He carried her; that's not hard to figure out. She was likely dead long before she got to the barn; he wasn't a large enough man to carry and hoist a live and thrashing grown woman. The bruising on her neck could have been due to the rope, but it was most likely from his hand. After he strangled her, he knew the best way to cover it up was to feign suicide by hanging. Right around the time Minnie was hanged, my brother's barn, a little over a mile away, burned to the ground. Minnie's farm was just on the edge of town, close enough for several townspeople to be able to see the yard and hear the goings-on there. Before he attempted the cover-up, he made sure any potential witnesses were distracted by the necessity of a bucket brigade.

The items left in her bedroom were the puzzle. Two knives were found in her bedroom. Kitchen knives, but sharp. These would explain the slight scratch on her neck I suppose, but he had a straight razor, too. Did he threaten her with it? If those knives had not been there, it would all be much easier to figure out. A pillow lay in a corner of the floor next to a hand mirror and a basin of water, slightly pink. Also lying close by, a towel. No matter how many times I tried to put him in that room with those things, I couldn't make sense of it. The placement of the pillow was deliberate, not tossed

haphazardly or flung in the midst of a struggle. The mirror and basin of water were near it, as if Minnie had been sitting on the pillow and gazing into the mirror. Why sit there? Why not sit at the vanity, which had its own mirror and comfortable chair? And what in the world was she doing? Most horrid to think of were the knives. The thing that's hard to say: Was she trying to commit suicide before he got to her? Or were the knives used as protection against him? Did she know he was coming? If so, why didn't she call anyone? If they were used as protection, then why the pillow and basin of water?

Like as not, I'll never piece that together.

The Brownfield case added another mystery to my file. I knew who killed them, but some things about it didn't make sense.

The thing that bothered me was Brownfield's reaction to Cerone. Why was he so adamant about keeping the gang away from the Kaufmans? That question was answered by digging into his past. Though Homer Brownfield was no tough guy, his father was involved with a gang that ran stolen cattle through the stockyards in Omaha, Nebraska. Turns out, one of the shipments of cattle was stolen from a Chicago gang who had done the same thing. In retaliation for taking what they deemed was theirs, the Chicago gang sent a hit man to Omaha to send a clear message.

In 1894, a group of 2,000 homeless men, called Kelly's army, stormed Omaha's Union Stockyards looking for supplies. During the unrelated chaos, Homer's father and two other Omaha gang members were shot and killed. Chicago made themselves known and vowed no further retaliation as long as their cattle shipments went unmolested in the future. Fifteen at the time, Brownfield was torn by a sense of revenge and a desire to distance himself completely from his father's connections. When he was old enough,

Brownfield learned veterinary science and worked in the stockyards checking cattle for disease. For a time, Brownfield maintained an excellent reputation. One incident, however, would turn that all around.

Brownfield approved for slaughter a shipment of cattle that was unfit for human consumption. Though there were no obvious outward signs, the animals were plagued with a bacterium that subsequently killed a dozen people in Omaha and Iowa and made countless others ill. The accident was fairly common in those days, but Brownfield's reputation as an honest veterinarian was sullied. People who knew Homer Brownfield's father and his connection with the Omaha gang, assumed Homer was in cahoots with the gang as well and that he signed off on the cattle for gang profit. He couldn't escape that reputation unless he really did escape, so he and his wife moved to Low Moor, Iowa, establishing a new store and a new life.

That night the Kaufmans struck a deal with Carmine Sabella. The Chicago gang didn't just strengthen revenue. Sabella and his associates covered up all evidence of foul play. They drove off that November night with four vehicles, theirs, the two autos the Klansmen had driven to Hurstville, and Cerone's. In the back of one was the prisoner. Sabella promised there would be no trouble from the authorities in regard to what happened to Cerone or the Klansmen that night, and if there was, the Chicago gang would take care of it.

Though the infamous Al Capone was part of the Chicago gang at that time, he wasn't in charge yet; that didn't happen until 1925 following an attack on Johnny Torrio's life. Tasting death, Torrio passed his legacy on to Capone. Despite the new leadership, the deal the Kaufmans struck with the

Chicago Outfit lasted until the end of Prohibition in 1933. The gang could easily have wrestled control of eastern Iowa distribution away from the family in addition to taking a piece of their sales. Perhaps they were distracted by another Iowa distiller. Templeton Rye gained quick favor with Capone, who would drink only what he deemed "the good stuff" instead of the watered-down and compromised Canadian whiskey his gang was notorious for distributing. Whatever the reason, the Kaufmans stayed rather unmolested during the era. The siblings stepped up production to meet additional demand, and all of Hurstville stayed afloat for a while. Wild River Whiskey never gained the notoriety of Templeton Rye, but something tells me that's just the way the Kaufmans wanted it.

The Volstead Act allowed for three exceptions to the Eighteenth Amendment. One of those exceptions was the administration of alcohol for medicinal purposes; licensed physicians and dentists could write prescriptions for hard liquor. Wild River Whiskey was good for several things that ailed you, from a simple cough to the prevention of cancer, according to a brochure produced and distributed approximately three months after the Kaufmans' business meeting with the Chicago Outfit. For old age, a doctor from Chicago was known to prescribe Kaufman whiskey as such: "Imbibe three ounces every hour until spirits rise." Ahem. Needless to say, such physicians were very much in demand.

The simple canning jar with the honeybee tag remained, though a sticker with a list of treatable ailments was added along with a prominent "For Medicinal Purposes" at the top.

The Kaufmans continued to sell their Wild River Whiskey to locals; Chicago never tried to touch that, as far as I know. There was a bubble around a tri-county area that remained impermeable as long as the whiskey river flowed east. The whiskey sold locally, was traditionally bottled, and looked like honey if one didn't examine it too closely.

Sometime after the Honey Whiskey Murders, I learned that certain plants have evolved to drug their nectar in order to attract bees. Since they are laced with caffeine, nicotine, or other chemicals, the bees come back for more. Who can say if the Kaufman bees were drawn to such plants, but the people who drank Wild River Whiskey were certainly drawn to its taste.

A honeybee has no secrets. A forager's story precedes her, pollen clinging to her legs and underbelly—a temporary tattoo of *here's where I've been, here's what I found, and here's what I did.* That pollen is a vital prologue for the bee larvae, who need its nutrients to grow and, in turn, to support the hive. Nectar, the heart of the tale, rests in the forager's stomach until she returns to the hive where she will share it with a house bee. It is then stored in a cell, and once sufficiently dehydrated, it becomes honey for all.

Pheromones don't lie, and these are the honeybee's greatest communication tools. Like telepathy, the pheromones move wavelike through the colony inciting action. Fight, forage, produce, change, clean, swarm. Multitudes of bees sing each other's stories in a natural harmony meant to ensure the existence of the colony. No single bee takes precedence. Not even the queen. If she is false or fading, they will depose her. They who will be dead in a day, a month, a season, don't just act for the living. They act for those that haven't even been born.

The afternoon shimmered in the hot sun of late July. My vision was blurred by heat waves rising over wildflowers and grasses. The bees busied themselves, walking daintily over circles of Queen Anne's Lace and nearly disappearing against the dark centers of Black-Eyed Susans. Suspended between tall stalks of big bluestem, a bright yellow and black garden spider waited for a meal while clinging to the center of its web. It came in the form of a horsefly, fat and juicy, nearly strong enough to break through the web altogether, but not quite.

I didn't mention the spider to Walter, just watched it work the fly into a sticky ball to be devoured later.

"Are you listening?" Walter said.

"What?"

"There he is."

"Mmm hmmm." The goings-on of the little creatures were far more interesting than the suspect we were shadowing. He followed a predictable schedule, meeting his contact on a park bench in Davenport every Saturday at 3:00.

Walter and I had spread a blanket under a shade tree at Vander Veer Park and pretended to read.

The contact sat down next to him. He had a little dog in tow that barked at our suspect incessantly. They quickly exchanged packages and the contact was on his way.

"Any regrets?" I asked Walter.

"Regrets?"

Though I didn't explain it to him, my question asked two things: Do you regret taking on the new job? Do you regret your relationship with me? My past was a wild and muddy Iowa river. There was the whole thing with Minnie, but Walter and I had that in common. I had something more troublesome churning in the waters of my past—the ghost of the man I had killed in that Minneapolis alley— something I hadn't told anyone. "About taking the job," I said.

Walter kept his eyes on the suspect. "Not one."

"Days like this aren't very exciting."

"It'll pick up. I know it's not always going to be like this."

The suspect stood and tucked his shirttail into his pants, adjusted his hat.

"Most of the days are like this, really," I said.

"What have you been thinking about, anyway? You've been off in your own world somewhere."

"I've been thinking about bees."

"Bees?"

"Walter, if we're going to survive together, in this job and in this life, we can't have any secrets."

As the suspect walked away, Walter and I rose and packed up our things. We followed him until he reached his home four blocks away and disappeared inside.

"Why this talk of secrets?" Walter asked.

"Because before we can go any further, I need to tell you something."

ACKNOWLEDGEMENTS

Abundant thanks go to:

Kris McGuire, for assisting in research. All of the articles I used came from your early library search, and our jaunt to the courthouse for those court records was morbidly fun.

Paul Ingram, book seller extraordinaire from the land of Prairie Lights, for taking a chance on that first book. Your encouragement means more than you can know.

Roger Hill, for being a bastion of local knowledge and for sharing crime scene details that went unreported in the papers. I'll never look at vanilla ice cream the same way again.

Kim Hess, Clinton County Clerk of Court, for tracking down those old court records in the dusty archives of the courthouse.

Bob Osterhaus, for giving me a slice of history to toy around with. Our lunch at Flapjacks is a fond memory, and your information on bootlegging in Hurstville spun me off in an unforeseen but welcome direction.

The volunteers at the Jackson County Historical Society and employees of The Hurstville Interpretive Center, for maintaining the archives. The myriad pictures of old Hurstville, the map of the place, and the firsthand accounts helped immensely in inspiring this fiction.

Dr. Michael Woltman, MD, for allowing me to watch during the autopsy. I may have ruined my relationship with lavender oil, but what I learned that day reached far beyond my expectations. You are an excellent teacher.

Dr. Eric Peterson, Clinton County Medical Examiner, for that early morning phone call that, at first, made me regret my request to view an autopsy.

Beekeeper Will Davis, for taking me out to see your bees in the Maquoketa area and showing me how incredibly beautiful they are. I fell in love with bees that day.

Beekeepers Don Clapp and Bill Smet, also Dianne and Neal Rinehard, for showing me the honey-harvesting process and for the gift of honey.

Andrea Wilson, for being such a great support system for Iowa Writers. Love to my Iowa City home away from home.

To the faculty at the Lindenwood MFA in Writing program, especially Tony D'Souza, for cultivating a warm and supportive environment and for all your excellent feedback.

My mom, Pat Frey, for assisting in the research process. One of my favorite pictures is of you "behind bars" at the West Branch bootlegging exhibit. We know how to have fun, don't we?

My dad, Gene Frey, for that honey whiskey afternoon and one weird coincidence. I'll never forget you just so happened to buy honey whiskey on the same day I decided honey would be the secret ingredient. Cheers!

And to both of you for being my best beta readers.

To the best mother-in-law anyone could ever have, Elaine, for helping to take care of the family.

To the hubs, Eddie, for many nights of brainstorming and problem solving and for being so incredibly cool about my time-consuming hobby.

To my four sons, for understanding my need to dive headfirst into another time and for always being the greatest fuel in my fire.

To Christine Gilroy, for late night editing sessions, magazine subscriptions, connections, encouragement, marketing ideas, grammar lessons, and laughs. You are marvelous!

ABOUT THE AUTHOR

Staci Mercado won a Midwest Book Award for her historical fiction novel, *Seeking Signs* (Four Feathers Press, 2013). She has published work in *Barely South Review*, *Flash Fiction Magazine*, and *Broad Street*. With an MFA in Creative Writing, Staci teaches writing at her local high school, youth workshops at the Iowa Writers' House in Iowa City, and was awarded the 2017 Outstanding Literary Arts Educator Award from the Midwest Writing Center.